EMPTY WORLD

2

BEYOND THE PORTAL

DAVID K. ANDERSON

THE EMPTY WORLD

BOOK 2

BEYOND
THE PORTAL

DAVID K. ANDERSON

Magical Scrivener Press
22 Hawkstead Hollow
Nashua, NH 03063

www.magicalscrivener.com

Publisher's Note: This is a work of fiction. Names, characters, places, and incidents are a product of the author's imagination. Locales and public names are sometimes used for atmospheric purposes. Any resemblance to actual people, living or dead, or to businesses, companies, events, institutions, or locales is completely coincidental.

Ordering Information: Special discounts are available on quantity purchases by corporations, associations, and others. For details, contact the publisher at the address above.

David K. Anderson – First Edition

ISBN 978-1-939233-90-5

Printed in the United States of America

For Kristin, Justin and Matthew

Thanks to Elizabeth Webster and to the Gayhardts, Vicki and Mike, for their invaluable help in understanding some of the unique talents, personalities, traits and challenges of people with autism and Asperger's syndrome. Without their guidance I would have been completely out of my depth in creating the character of Brad.

That being said, I went on my own flights of fancy with the character, so if anything does not ring true, the responsibility falls squarely on me.

CHAPTER 1

Christy Walker wasn't happy, but she'd been expecting the contentious discussion with her parents for months. It was May and the living room was flooded with warm sunlight. The cattails on the edge of the pond down the hill were now two feet high and the geese had landed and would stay for a few weeks as they did every year. By this time of the season, the spring peepers were winding down their choruses and the bullfrogs were replacing them. All the signs of the pond coming back to life after the hard New Hampshire winter were visible from where Christy and her mom and dad were standing. Christy suspected her parents chose to confront her with the pond in view to emphasize their point.

It was almost inevitable that her parents would take this opportunity once the windows were open to the fresh air and sunlight, and she'd been waiting for it and dreading it. Her mom and dad had been at it for the better part of five minutes when Christy interrupted them.

"Mom, Dad!" Christy said, looking from one to the other. "I know. You don't have to have this discussion with me." Fourteen-year-old Christy plopped herself down on her living room couch, the same one she'd been sitting on her whole life, from when the house had been her grandmother's. Christy's parents had owned the house since her grandmother had died from cancer the year before. Her parents had kept most of the furniture in the room, deciding not to change how it looked, which was the same as it had looked for as long as Christy could remember.

Christy deliberately turned away from the pond down the hill and folded her arms across her chest, pouting because of the way the discussion was going and trying hard to hold back tears.

Her dad began pacing back and forth across the room and spoke up before her mom could respond.

"Yes we do, Christy. It's the end of May and we just had our first thunderstorm of the season. We've tried very hard not to harp on this all winter, but now that it's a real threat again, we just wanted to remind you." He stopped pacing and sat down in the chair facing the couch, leaning forward to point his finger at her. "And *you* don't seem to realize the seriousness of the situation we could face every time there's a thunderstorm. You and your friends and who knows how many others now know about the portal. It's a dangerous thing."

Christy rolled her now tearing-up blue eyes and tuned her dad out.

"Don't ignore me, young lady!" he shouted.

Christy's mom took her dad's hands in hers, patting them then holding on tight, and calmly took over the discussion.

"Honey, I know you, Trevor, and Danny have spent a lot of time together this past winter, and I think that's been wonderful. Danny looks up to you and idolizes Trevor, and I think it's marvelous that he's continued to teach you and Trevor signing, and that you've both responded enthusiastically to it. I get all that.

"But I also know you, and you haven't given up trying to convince us to let you go searching for your grandfather ... which leads me to think that part of the reason you three use sign language is to hide what you're saying from your father and I."

Christy stomped her foot, the tears flowing freely now. "No, that's not true!" she yelled. "After all that time with Danny in the Empty World, I realized how important signing can be, that's all. And Danny's now in Trev's scout troop so Trev wants to learn too."

Her mom smiled at her, hesitating and then shaking her head, and Christy knew she wasn't buying the argument. At the pause in conversation, her dad stood up, full of anxious energy, and began pacing again before slipping behind the couch to stare out the window at the pond, the object at the center of their discussion.

Christy stared through teary eyes at her mom and then at her dad, who was still gazing out the window. She kept silent.

"Honey, I do understand," her mom pressed on. "Believe me, I do. He's my father and until you came back from the Empty World, I thought he was dead—we all did."

"But we don't know if he's still alive!" Christy shouted, slapping the couch cushions. "The ancients may have killed him. There was no way he could escape them when we took off in the glider. He's either dead or they captured him." She sobbed, waiting for her mom or dad to respond.

Her dad turned around and stared directly at her. "With the first thunderstorm already come and gone, there's now going to be numerous times that the portal will open up. You," he said, pointing at her for emphasis, "stay away from the pond. Understood?"

Christy just sat there, gripping the edge of the seat cushion with her hands and crying. Her dad opened his mouth to speak again, but her mom held up her hand to stop him. "I promise we won't bring this up again all summer," she said, "... as long as you do just what your father said ... stay away from the pond. No secret plans for rescue or anything. Ok?"

Christy didn't respond. Her mom's eyes narrowed and the smile she'd had for most of the conversation disappeared. "This isn't a game," she said.

Christy frowned and leaned forward, angrily gripping the couch cushions. "I know, Mom. I was there," she snapped. She threw herself back, folded her arms across her chest and waited. Biting her lip, she tried to gage her mother's reaction. She never talked to her mom like that, and it gave her a little thrill. When her mom didn't show anger or annoyance, Christy tried to press what she hoped was a small advantage.

"How can you not know what's happened to him and just accept that?" she asked.

Her mom looked at her, frowning slightly, her eyes softening. Christy knew that look meant she was going to say something that Christy wouldn't like but that she felt her pain too. "If there was a way for your grandfather to get back to us, he'd try if he really wanted to. He had years to decide to try to come home. It's been over nine months. We have to accept that there is nothing we can do. If we haven't gotten a call from France— and we haven't— either he's ok and doesn't want to get back here, or he can't get back here."

"Exactly, Mom. If he can't, he needs help," Christy said, wiping her eyes.

Her dad grunted in response, and her mother once again looked at him, pleading with him to stay quiet on the issue. She then took Christy's hand, seemingly struggling to find words. "Maybe he does need help," she said finally, "but it won't be you, or any of us. End of discussion."

Christy pulled her hand away and stood up. She looked from her mom to her dad and back again, then bolted out of the living room.

Upstairs in her bedroom, Christy sat on her bed, trying to calm herself down. She needed to call Trevor. Not only was he the only one who would understand, but it concerned him personally too. She took her cell phone out and called him.

"It's me," she said when she heard him pick up.

"What's up?" Trevor asked.

"I'm so glad you finally got a cell phone." On the other end, Trevor laughed. "My parents were at me again about my grandfather," she said. "And my mom and Mrs. Lake figured out why we don't go over Danny's."

There was silence on the other end for a few seconds. "Does it change anything?" Trevor asked.

"I guess not." Christy was suddenly cautious, worried about being overheard. She jumped up from the bed and opened her door, but the corridor was empty.

"Christy? You there?" Trevor asked.

"Sorry, I had to make sure they're not listening. You know my parents will be watching me like a hawk now. I wouldn't be surprised if they tried to lock me in my room during thunderstorms." She sighed.

"If they catch you even looking towards the pond in bad weather, they just might try that," Trevor agreed, chuckling. "What if you're not home during a storm … or if they think you're not home? They wouldn't be paying attention to the pond then, would they?"

"If they think I'm with you or Danny, it won't matter. They'll still be cautious," she reasoned.

"Then the plan has to include you being somewhere else, somewhere that they will feel comfortable that you won't be able to access the pond from. And somewhere Danny and I wouldn't be with you."

Christy thought over Trevor's idea. It seemed reasonable. "We'll have to plan something so that they think I'm with someone they can trust. I don't know who that might be though. Ginny, Rob, or even the twins would still make them suspicious."

Trevor laughed. "You're probably right. If you started hanging around Cory, your parents would definitely suspect an ulterior motive." Trevor paused. "What about Brad by himself?"

"I don't know. He's come a few times with Danny to learn sign language with us. I'm not sure that my parents would think he's any safer to be with than anyone else who knows about the portal. Brad may be strange, but he's really a nice guy. Mom wouldn't mind me hanging with him if Cory wasn't around, but my parents probably think he's as big a risk as you or Danny or Ginny. Plus, according to you, he likes me. My mom might think I could convince him to lie for us."

"Then it has to be someone who your parents think doesn't know anything about the portal or what happened last year," Trevor said. "Gotta go, someone's coming."

Christy didn't have time to say goodbye before Trevor hung up. She stood in her room thinking about what he'd just suggested and realized he was on to something. But who fit the criteria? Who did she know who had no knowledge of the portal, or that she, Danny, and Rob had spent a week in another world that they'd accessed through it? Nobody that she could think of at the moment.

Cory Peters was enormously enjoying his time by himself, because he knew it was not going to last. He had to savor every minute. His mom wasn't currently after him to see to his brother's needs, but that was only because Brad wasn't home. As soon as Brad came back from Danny's house, Cory knew he'd be playing nursemaid to him as always.

While he had some peace and quiet, Cory reached under his bed and dragged out the backpack he kept hidden there. He took out the piece of paper he had looked at so many times and unfolded it carefully. Rob had made the sketch from memory. It was a drawing of a puzzle door, the puzzle door that Rob, Danny and Christy had solved to get through the portal and back to France. Cory smiled. Rob wouldn't have given it to him willingly. He was still pissed off at Cory for pushing him into the portal. That's why Cory had needed to take it from his brother. Rob must have given it to Brad while they were studying sign language at Christy's house, and Cory had stolen the original sketch from Brad's backpack months ago to copy it.

Now he studied the sketch, marveling at the detail. Rob was good, but he had never let him know it. Not that Rob would talk to him again anyway. But Rob loved talking to Brad about his time in what Christy called the Empty World. And Brad, though he seldom showed real enthusiasm, always came home and told him about it all with a little prompting. Sometimes it took a lot more than a little prompting, but Cory knew his brother's peculiar ways and had certainly perfected the art of getting Brad to give a blow by blow account of who said what— even to the point of him speaking each person's sentences as if he were that person.

That little group learning sign language from Danny was Cory's ticket to all the information about the Empty World that he wanted ... as long as he could keep Brad telling him about it as if he were a tape recorder. Not even their mom could get Brad to talk so much.

Cory rolled the drawing back up and stowed the backpack under his bed again, where he'd leave it until he needed it. The summer was almost here and, in a month or so, conditions would be right. He just had to keep telling Brad that both of them would go, so that the dimwit would keep plying Rob for information and keep their plans secret.

Cory had even convinced Brad that he would be in charge of taking the pictures that would make the two of them famous when they returned home. If Brad ever knew the truth, he'd go ballistic. But there was no way he was going to drag Brad along to be a liability while he documented the Empty World. He couldn't wait to actually see and photograph the insect-like alien called Clacker.

Cory heard the front door open and close and he groaned. Any second, he'd hear his mom scream his name and his time alone would be over. Brad was home.

CHAPTER 2

Connie Walker sat alone at the kitchen table. It was the same kitchen table that she had shared for so many years with her mom and dad. Spread across it were many photos of her dad's paintings of the Empty World, and the letters and other things that her mother had left for Christy. She slowly picked each of them up, in no particular order, and reverently placed them back down. She was crying again.

She ached to see her dad. At least once a day since she'd found out her dad had been alive all these years, Connie secretly took out the packet of things her mom had put together for Christy before she'd died. No amount of secretly looking at his photos and paintings could really lessen that ache, but since these tangible mementoes were all she had, she made the best of them.

No one knew about her daily routine—certainly not Christy. If she ever found out, Connie knew she'd use the weakness against her and try even harder. Connie wondered if Christy could eventually succeed, and desperately hoped the answer would always be no. But part of her wished she could have given Christy her blessing to go look for her dad. She would never say yes and risk losing her daughter, but she hated that the situation was bleak enough to make her consider it for even a second. She'd been lucky that Christy and her friends had come home safe from their time in that world. Christy could just as easily have never returned, and then she and Doug might never have known what had become of her. The thought was unbearable.

Still, knowing that her dad was alive was difficult to accept and to do nothing about. She felt a deep longing to see her dad again, which kept him haunting her dreams and her secretly stealing these moments every day. The worst part was that she knew she could never— *would* never go herself. And that made her admire Christy even more.

Connie lost track of time while sorting through the stack of amazing photos and letters in front of her. She didn't hear Doug walk in, and when she noticed him standing over her, she quickly wiped her eyes. Looking up at him, she tried to smile. It was the first time since the summer before that she'd let him see her crying over the collection of her dad's photos.

He sat down opposite her at the table and reached for her hand, squeezing it gently.

"I know this is hard for you." He paused, and Connie watched as he scanned the collection that was scattered on the table between them. "Maybe we should let the whole world know about the Empty World."

Connie shook her head. "Do you really want the world in our backyard?"

"Well, we wouldn't even have to tell anyone about our portal necessarily. We could tell them about the one in France and let the world gather around there. When enough people got to the Empty World, they'd be bound to find Jack, sooner or later," Doug reasoned.

Connie squeezed her husband's hand. "No, my mom was right. It should remain a secret if we can help it. Though we may not be able to keep it secret for much longer anyway. In our town alone, there are too many of us who know about it, never mind the village in France we traveled to. And who knows how many other portals there might be, on how many other worlds. According to the kids, dad thought that Clacker came from somewhere else and wasn't originally from the Empty World.

"So, if it gets out somehow, maybe I will see my dad again. But if nobody slips up, then these things are all I'll ever have," she said, gesturing at the mementoes spread out upon the table. "I have to accept that, I guess." She started sobbing and Doug came around the table to stand behind her, putting his arms around her shoulders. She leaned into the comforting embrace and cried even harder.

"Cory, does mom know?" Brad asked. Cory was sitting on his bed, trying to ignore his pestering brother who asked the same question at least two or three times a day.

"No, idiot, if she did, she'd be screaming at us and would have told dad about it ages ago. So shut up. You don't want mom to overhear us." Cory turned his back again and picked up his comic book, hoping this time it would stop Brad's questions.

Cory felt his stare but refused to make eye contact. Not that Brad would actually make eye contact, anyway. If Cory did turn around Brad would just avert his gaze, so what was the point? Cory buried his head in the comic book he was trying to read.

After a moment of silence, Cory chanced a quick look and found Brad still staring at him. Cory shook his head. When they were younger, and Cory had noticed Brad staring at him as he was now, he made a game of staring back, which immediately got Brad to drop his eyes. Then Cory would go back to doing something else until Brad stared at him again. Cory would let this go on and on until he got tired of teasing Brad or until their mom walked in and realized what he was doing. Now he didn't usually tease Brad that way; he'd found a number of different ways that weren't so obvious.

After all these years, he still couldn't get used to his brother's peculiar ways. Even though his mom explained it to him almost weekly, Cory still had trouble grasping the fact that Brad was very different than he was, despite being his twin. When they were younger, Cory had just accepted Brad's differences. But ever since the doctors had said that Brad had Asperger's syndrome, Cory had struggled with understanding what that meant. Well, he knew what some of it meant— it meant that he always had to watch out for Brad and endure their mom constantly harping on him to take care of him. That's what it meant. And he was getting fed up with it.

"Cory?"

"What now, Brad?" Cory asked, still trying to focus on his comic book.

"Are you sure?"

Cory slapped down the comic book. "Sure, about what?" Cory was never certain exactly what Brad was referring to when he asked questions like that. He could have been talking about almost anything.

"I want to go through the portal. You pushed Rob into the pond. Are you going to jail?"

"Brad, don't say that again. He's home safe now. And he fell into the pond."

"You pushed him," Brad stated.

"Christy's been lying to you when you practice sign language with her, Brad. She has you convinced that you saw something you didn't, that's all."

"Christy didn't lie. I was there. I saw you."

Brad frowned and hesitated, as always, and Cory knew that it meant he was going to keep on asking the same questions and saying the same things over and over again, no matter how angry Cory got, or how much he yelled and called Brad as many bad names as he could think of before their mom got involved. Or like was happening more and more now, Brad would start signing to nobody in particular, wrapped in his own world.

Cory tried a new tactic— one that he knew would get some type of reaction out of Brad.

"Brad, if you don't stop asking me about going to the Empty World every chance you get, I'm going to go alone and leave you here," Cory said.

"No, you promised we'd go," Brad replied.

"Yes, but I might change my mind if you don't stop asking all the time."

"You promised."

"I take it back, then," Cory growled.

"You promised."

Cory gave up, tired of the back and forth. He reached for his comic book again and tried to ignore Brad completely.

Instead of continuing to pester him, Brad sat down at their desk and busied himself with his notebook. As soon as Cory saw that, he lost interest in what Brad was doing and gratefully focused on reading.

Cory had almost forty-five minutes of peace. In that time, he'd read two comics and was about to start a third when he looked up to see Brad standing over him with a couple of sheets of drawing paper in his hand. Without saying a word, Brad offered the papers to Cory, who took them with a frown.

"Brad? What are these?"

Brad just stood there, not making eye contact, only staring at his own hands clasped in front of him and shifting his weight back and forth in a rocking motion. Cory tried to figure out the best way to get a useful response from him as he took a closer look at the drawings.

"Did you just draw these?" he finally asked, real admiration in his voice.

Brad nodded then offered, "We'll have to come through those doors to get back home."

"Home? What—" As it dawned on Cory what the sketches were, their mom walked in. Cory handed them to her. "Did you know Brad could draw this good?"

"Well," Mrs. Peters said, correcting Cory's grammar. She glanced at the drawings and then at Brad, who just stood there rocking gently, not reacting to either Cory's comments or their mom entering the room.

"He used to draw a lot when you both were little, but I haven't seen him do this in years." She handed the drawings to Cory and asked, "What are these?"

"They're pictures of the portal doors that Christy, Danny and Rob went through to get back to France."

"How did Brad know what they looked like?" Mrs. Peters asked.

"Don't know. Maybe Rob made his own drawings and Brad just remembered enough to copy them," Cory suggested.

"Brad can do some amazing things from memory, so it wouldn't surprise me at all." As she said that, Brad stopped rocking and stepped closer to the bedroom window. He began signing furiously.

Mrs. Peters turned to him. "Brad, it's time to eat," she said gently. "Come away from the window." She left the room without waiting for a response. To Cory's surprise, Brad stopped his signing and followed her out.

Cory waited for a few seconds then sprang up off the bed and peeked out the bedroom door. He could hear his mom talking in the kitchen to Brad, so he took both drawings and put them side by side on the desk.

After a few minutes of studying them he took out his cell phone and snapped a few quick pictures of each. Then, making sure he still heard his mom and Brad in the kitchen, he slipped both sketches into his and Brad's printer and made a copy of each. He wondered if his mom had noticed that the drawings were vastly different. One was clearly of the doors with the wooden blocks in their correct positions, as they had been after Rob solved the puzzle to get the doors open. They created a picture of some type of city. The other one had the blocks in different positions, scrambled and making little sense. Either Rob really had made his own sketches from memory and Brad had copied them, or Rob had such a real talent for description—and an amazing memory himself—that Brad was able to create his sketches of the doors from those descriptions.

Cory smiled to himself as he stowed the copies he'd just made in his backpack— the backpack he was slowly preparing for his trip through the portal. He hoped that Rob and Danny were telling Brad the truth about their experiences in the Empty World. If Brad continued to believe that he and Cory were going to go there, then he would continue to tell Cory everything he knew, and Cory would continue to take it all in. When he went through Christy's portal alone, he'd be prepared for whatever was there to greet him.

Then for the hundredth time or so since he'd thought up his plan to go, he imagined the news stations interviewing him on his return after publishing all the photos and videos he'd take. If nobody else wanted to take credit for finding the place, he'd do it gladly. Then he'd be too busy with all the worldwide attention for his mom to hassle him about Brad. For that matter, with all the money he'd get for his story—maybe he'd write a book to go along with the photos— his mom could hire someone to look after Brad, someone who was trained to do it. It was a win, win.

CHAPTER 3

Brad sat on the edge of his bed practicing his signing and mumbling to himself. "Cory says I'm not going. But he promised. I'll go first and meet him there. Then he can't say no."

He looked over at his sleeping brother. He hoped Cory wouldn't wake up. Cory almost never did when he was up talking. On the few occasions when Cory ever did wake up, he'd just shake his head and roll over trying to get back to sleep. But Brad felt he had to be more quiet tonight.

He wasn't reciting his favorite movie, word for word, or his favorite book like he usually did. If Cory woke up now, he'd probably realize that it wasn't what their mom called "scripting" that Brad was doing.

Instead of going right back to sleep, he might listen more closely.

Outside his window the rain was coming down in sheets. It had taken years, but he finally could listen to the pelting water against the windows and not curl up into a defensive crouch with his hands tightly clamped over his ears. With the help of all the specialists and his mom, he had learned to focus on other things than the sounds that made his senses go into overload. He would never really like the rain, but it was more tolerable now than it had been. The thought that he would have to walk out onto Christy's dock in a storm to go to the Empty World still scared him, but he already knew what he would focus on. He'd committed three different Robert Louis Stevenson tales to memory for frightening moments, and he planned to recite one to himself. He was particularly fond of Treasure Island, and that's the one he thought he'd use.

It was the middle of June and Brad was through with school. Cory wasn't due to be out of school until several days, which Brad felt was good. From the minute Cory had threatened to go without him, he had planned to go on ahead and wait for Cory in the Empty World.

Brad had weather patterns printed out and pinned up on the wall behind the desk. The current storm forecast was represented on one of the printed sheets. Brad had added comments in black marker that hinted clearly at his plans and didn't think to hide them. Cory had seen them on the wall but never bothered to look more closely. Other than berating Brad about wasting the colored ink, Cory ignored them as he did with almost everything that Brad did in their room. Brad had even circled on his calendar the times that the weather patterns might produce thundershowers in the coming week. Tonight could be it.

Brad stopped his signing and took out his backpack. His mom had picked it out especially for him years before. It was real canvas with raised stitching, unlike most of the packs that were nylon or some other synthetic cloth. Brad couldn't stand those other materials touching his skin, but he loved the feel of the canvas and the seams, so neatly stitched.

Taking it out and placing its full weight in his lap was part of his daily routine now. There really was nothing he needed to do with it. He'd had it ready for weeks. He just sat hugging it to his chest as he slowly rocked forward and back, listening to the rhythmic sound of Cory's sleeping.

He waited just to be certain that Cory was soundly asleep and quietly slipped out of the room. His parents both were sound sleepers, especially since his mom had stopped the constant surveillance she had kept of the pond when Christy's grandmother was still alive. It made it simple for Brad to get outside just as the really heavy rain was starting and the lightning and thunder were not far off. He headed quickly down to the pond.

Brad had been there before, although at the time, he'd had no idea of the portal's existence. That was the night that Cory had pushed Rob into the pond as the portal opened up, but Brad didn't like thinking about that. Tonight, he knew what to expect and stood waiting with his backpack clutched tightly in his arms. Knowing what to expect when the portal opened because he'd seen it before was a huge plus for him. If Cory wasn't with him as he had been the first time *and* he didn't know what to expect, he'd be curled up, silently whining or possibly screaming. But he did know what to expect, and reciting Treasure Island to himself also helped him not be afraid.

He also had noise protectors over his ears as he'd been told to do, and he'd been practicing getting used to the way they felt on his head for a while. They still annoyed him, but they kept the noise of the storm muffled, and his reciting helped him fight the urge to rip them off.

He waited.

Danny had nightmares. They were worse during bad weather like tonight, and he was afraid he might never stop having them. They had plagued him ever since his return from the Empty World. Unlike Christy, who constantly talked about trying to go back to the Empty World, Danny had no such desire.

He knew of Christy's and Trevor's plan to sneak back. They'd spoken often of it during their meetings with him to learn sign language. But every chance he got, Danny made it clear that he didn't approve and wouldn't even think of going back himself.

Now Brad had let it slip that he and Cory were planning to go there also. With the beginning of the summer storms and his continuing nightmares, Danny was reluctant to fall asleep, instead choosing to try to stay awake by watching out the window for signs of a thunderstorm. In two days when school was out for the year, he'd have to stay awake even more often. So far, he hadn't seen any signs that Christy and Trevor or Cory and Brad were hanging around the dock. But Danny was pretty sure that Mrs. Walker was keeping a close watch on Christy. He wasn't so sure about who might be watching out for the twins though.

Even if he did happen to see someone down by the dock in a thunderstorm, he didn't really have a plan. He supposed that he'd try to get down there and talk whoever it was out of going if he could. He even had a backpack ready to go, not for himself though. If he couldn't stop someone from going, he planned to give them his pack. He was pretty sure his pack was better stocked than any that Cory or Brad would throw together.

Pulling his desk chair quietly over to the window, he settled down in it, leaned his crossed arms on the sill, then rested his chin down, nose pressed to the glass. Tonight was a perfect night to focus on the pond. It was warm, the rain was just beginning, and heat lightning was periodically illuminating the sky. The only downside was that he still had to go to school tomorrow.

Danny was starting to nod off, but each time, he snapped back awake with a start. This time as he forced his eyes open, he saw the pond lit up in the distance by a bright flash of lightning. In the white spotlight, the pond was an angry, swirling mass of choppy water, and the dock cast a black shadow across a third of its width. Suddenly Danny noticed a shadow stretching over the dock and gyrating across the water. He couldn't believe his eyes.

Danny waited. He was wide awake now. At the next lightening flash, he confirmed it— someone was on the dock!

He hoped his mom was asleep as he grabbed his pack, pulled a coat on, and snuck quietly out the door. Once out, he bolted as fast as he could down towards the pond and the figure on the dock.

While he was still fifty or so yards away, he groaned. A lightning strike hit the pond just right and Danny knew what that would mean. It also showed him who was on the dock— it was Brad. As Danny reached the dock and started to catch up, Brad jumped. Danny got to the end of the dock while the yellow swirls were still gyrating below him. He knew enough from the last few months to know that Brad was the worst possible person he could have seen all alone on the dock. Brad had many unusual skills, but Danny was afraid that being able to cope with finding himself in an unfamiliar and dangerous world wasn't among them. Making a quick decision, he leaped out into the yellowish swirling caldron, where seconds before there had been only pond water, and followed Brad to the Empty World.

CHAPTER 4

Christy tossed and turned as the storm passed overhead. She'd had trouble sleeping during thunderstorms ever since she had returned from the Empty World. Part of it was because she hated the lost opportunities. Tonight, she lay fully awake in bed, focused on the sounds outside. Thunder echoed as the rain pelted her windows. The room lit up with each flash of lightning. Christy turned over, determined to block it all out and get back to sleep, but a familiar ache haunted her.

Once the storms woke her up, it was the wondering that kept her awake. Where was her grandfather now? No matter what she did to distract herself, she couldn't keep from wondering. Tonight was no different.

Another rumble of thunder coincided with a gust of wind that threw an angry sheet of rain against her window. But there was something else in that last wind gust. Something that shouldn't be there, not in this weather, and she came instantly back to full consciousness. Her window was being opened!

Christy slept with a small nightlight from her childhood. As she sat up alarmed, that small light provided enough illumination to see her window slide up slowly. She looked around in a panic for something to use to protect herself. Since her room was on the second floor, whoever was opening the window had gone to some trouble to do so. Finding nothing close by to use as a weapon, she slid down off her bed and hid behind it.

As the gusting wind blew the rain in, causing her curtains to flap violently, the figure awkwardly trying to crawl into her room was partially obscured. She spoke loudly, trying to sound as threatening as she could to whomever it was coming in.

"Whoever you are, I'm going to scream." Then a hopeful thought came to her. "Trev? Is that you?" For a frightening heartbeat the intruder was silent, and Christy stood up ready to bolt for her doorway and let loose the threatened scream.

"You're kidding, Walker, right? Does Hanson do this often?"

Relief caused the tension to drain from her body. Christy couldn't believe it. It was Cory. All she could muster for a response was, "What are you doing here?"

Cory, catching a foot on the sill, tumbled onto the floor, saying something under his breath as he fell.

"Close the window, you jerk," Christy snapped.

Cory stood up. "You're coming with. Get dressed. We're going to the Empty World."

Christy just stood there. The whole situation was just too much; she struggled to process it all.

"Come on! Brad's jumped into the portal," Cory said, the words coming out high and squeaky— very unlike the Cory she knew. He took his cap off and ran his hands through his hair, mumbling, "I'm so dead. She's going to murder me." Putting his cap back on, he spread his arms wide, palms extended towards her to emphasize his plea. "Listen, I woke up and Brad was missing. I looked out the window and he was about to jump into the pond."

A thrill quickly passed through her, but this was *Cory*. Her dislike and distrust got the better of her.

"Why should I help you?"

"Well, your little pal went in after him," Cory added, folding his arms across his chest and staring at her, his voice steadier.

"Danny?" Christy was stunned.

"Yeah, Flying Fingers himself. Let's go! Get moving. If we hurry, we might get a chance before the storm ends. Maybe the portal will open up again."

Any pretense of resistance was gone. Christy darted across the room and pulled some clothes out of her dresser. Cory waited, shifting from one foot to the other, and then paced in a small tight circle.

He seemed not to notice that he was soaked. Christy quickly got her clothes on right over her pajamas, and then grabbed her well prepared backpack out of its hiding spot.

"You have anything packed?" she asked.

"Yeah, I've got a pack on the ground below the ladder."

"Good, because I don't have enough to be sharing with you."

Cory wasn't paying attention. He had already bolted towards the blowing curtains and was climbing back out the window. Calling out over his shoulder, he repeated, "My mom will kill me if I don't find him."

Christy took a last look around the room, thrilled to be heading back to the Empty World ... even if it was with Cory, the last person in the world she would have chosen to go with, if she'd had a choice.

Danny was prepared for the jolt as he hit the ground. The wind was no surprise either. He picked himself up immediately after absorbing the shock and looked around for Brad.

Just down the slope a bit, Brad clearly hadn't been prepared for either the serious drop to the ground or the subsequent wind. He was curled up, his back to the main force of the gale. Danny hurried over and grabbed him by the arm, yanking him up rudely. Brad barely registered who it was urging him to get up, but he followed Danny anyway.

There was an opening just a little way ahead that Danny remembered, and he headed straight for it. Within a few minutes, he slipped into the opening, dragging Brad along with him by the arm. Once out of the wind, Danny stopped and sat down on the smooth floor of the tunnel they had taken refuge in. Brad followed suit. He tapped Brad on his ear protection and signed that he was safe to remove it.

Brad nodded and pulled his ear protection off. "Now I can wait for Cory," he said.

Danny hadn't expected Brad to say anything, so he hadn't paid attention to Brad's lips. "What?" he signed.

Brad repeated, "Now I can wait for Cory." Then he seemed to remember who he was talking with and signed also, but Danny had understood anyway.

"Cory's coming?" Danny signed and asked.

Brad nodded. "We planned it, but he said he was going to go without me. Now he can't. I'm going to wait for him here." Brad stared at Danny's hands, ignoring the strange tunnel around him.

"Does he know you came ahead of him?" Danny signed. Brad understood and shook his head no. Pounding his fists on the smooth surface of the tunnel floor, Danny stifled a frustrated scream.

Danny had only really met Brad after he had come back from the Empty World and started to teach Christy, Rob, and Trevor sign language. Brad had heard about it from Rob and joined in with their little group. Brad was the best at it of them all. In fact, Brad was amazing at it. He seemed to be more comfortable staring at people's hands than looking them in the eye. The only area where he fell behind the others was in interpreting facial expressions that were a part of many signs. And sometimes Danny didn't understand Brad's thinking ... how he went from point A to point B. This was one of those times.

Once Danny had found out that Brad had Asperger's, he had empathized with him. Even though they faced a different set of challenges, Danny tried hard to help Brad fit in during the impromptu sessions when he taught them all signing. And generally, Brad did fit in— especially when Christy was there.

But right now, Danny wasn't in any mood to empathize. He was upset. Brad's thinking process had landed him back in the Empty World. Of the half a dozen or so kids in town who knew about this place, Danny was the only one who didn't want to be here. Yet here he was. And the only way home for the two of them was a long way off.

Jack was worried. He'd been in prison in the village of the ancients since he'd tried to help his granddaughter and her friends get to the working portal. Based on the account of his imprisoned companions, CaTaz and PeSaz, the kids had successfully crossed through the portal back to Earth. Jack was relieved about that. But now new rumors about the ancient, TuMaz, had started to circulate. He'd been given some sort of military title and a small group to command. Apparently, their mission was to find and destroy Clacker and as many Cleaners as they encountered in the process. TuMaz hadn't come to torment Jack in days, which was very unlike the ancient. Something had to be up.

NaTaz, the jailor who passed these rumors on to them, seemed like a good enough sort and was never cruel to them. He was CaTaz's brother and Jack could tell this made him more sympathetic to them all. He wondered if NaTaz might turn out to be the weak link in their imprisonment. If Jack could get NaTaz to side with them against TuMaz and the rest of the village, it could be a way out. And Jack remembered the Orator's story of a Cleaner escaping the village through the help of an unknown ancient. Perhaps NaTaz was that ancient, though it seemed unlikely that he would still be the jailor if he'd let a prisoner escape.

Since Jack had been locked up, he had come to realize that his two cellmates, and probably the rest of the ancients in this village, were ignorant of the more advanced culture in their past. As far as Jack had been able to determine, only the Orator and Clacker knew anything about the history of this world which time had so inexorably erased. Jack suspected that even his two friends' knowledge was lacking, steeped more in legend than real history.

He was frustrated day after day at his helplessness to do anything, so he'd spent the better part of the past days and months learning the ancient's language from CaTaz and PeSaz, and to a lesser extent from NaTaz as well.

Since Jack now had a working knowledge of their language, he knew that CaTaz was constantly pleading all their cases to his brother. So far it hadn't had any visible effect, but Jack could only hope that eventually it would. Jack thought about the jailor. Standing guard over his own brother must have been difficult, no matter what that brother was accused of.

If NaTaz was right and TuMaz really was hunting Clacker down, Jack feared that war was imminent. He knew Clacker could take care of himself, but if TuMaz truly had a company of men at his command and they met others of Clacker's kind, it would go badly for the Cleaners. If he could warn Clacker, perhaps it would help stack the deck in his friend's favor. Of course, the ancients had always wanted to kill the Cleaners, but it concerned Jack even more now that a concerted effort was in motion.

Since first hearing of the rumors, Jack had been wracking his brain that much harder for a way to break out. So far, no opportunity had presented itself, but that didn't mean one wouldn't. He just had to be ready if and when one did.

Jack wasn't a particularly religious man, but the saying 'the Lord helps those who help themselves' had taken on a greater significance since his imprisonment. Even though he was currently powerless to escape, he'd been preparing daily to take advantage of any opportunity. Not knowing what that opportunity might be, he did whatever he could to cover any eventuality. Despite the restrictions his cramped quarters presented, he exercised his arms and legs every day. If he had to run or fight his way out, the last thing he wanted was to be weak and out of shape.

Jack had also fashioned a couple of sharp instruments from eating utensils he'd stolen. But the knives that the ancients used to spear solid food, Jack didn't dare swipe. The ancients who delivered and retrieved his meal trays would have noticed the absence of them. Metal was a precious commodity to the ancients, and although they gave him metal utensils, something as obvious as a knife would not be allowed to stay missing for long. Over the course of many, many meals, Jack had chanced to swipe two of the thin spoon-like utensils for eating liquids. The ancients retrieving his trays those nights had been particularly dimwitted, and the utensils hadn't been missed.

Over time Jack had ground the handles of both of them into very sharp points against the roughhewn stone of his cell's walls.

He'd also found that the hard, tasteless bread they gave him didn't spoil when it wasn't consumed right away. It got harder, but didn't mold, and as long as Jack wrapped it tightly with what little wrapping material he had, none of the insects constantly crawling over everything could get at it. Jack stashed this bread to take with him in the event he found an opening to make his escape. And really, he felt confident that he'd lived and survived long enough in this world that he could live off the land if need be.

Jack's thoughts were interrupted by approaching footsteps—footsteps that were different than the confident strides of TuMaz or the more deferential strides of NaTaz. These footsteps were lighter, and the owner seemed to hesitate as they got closer.

From around the bend in the corridor, an ancient slowly showed himself, hesitating and finally stopping well back from Jack's prison door. Peering through the small viewing slot, Jack was startled and amused to see such a young ancient, but he greeted him with deference.

"I honor your Ancestors in your presence," he said, bowing deeply to the startled ancient. A thick door separated them, but since Jack's head had momentarily disappeared from the small opening, the ancient saw that Jack had not only spoken the customary 'First Greeting' but had also followed it with the formal bow.

The ancient glanced behind him and back towards Jack several times before he seemingly remembered his manners.

"And I in your presence." The bow was exaggerated; the sweeping arm gesture that went along with it brushing the ancient's fingertips to the rough stone floor of the corridor.

With his response, the ancient seemed to gain some confidence and stood straight up, staring at Jack's face through the door, though he kept his distance.

"Come closer, friend. I don't get many visitors. Especially ones as young as you. You are?"

The ancient turned his head, glancing behind himself once more. Turning back to face Jack, he took a hesitant step forward.

"gi-BuMaz my father has named me, and I have honored him and my ancestors with it. And my clan is Tan."

Jack smiled, hoping the boy could see the universal gesture through the opening.

"Jack. Just 'Jack' my father has named me. And my clan is Renfrew." Then he reverted to English and said, "And I've made a mess of it in front of my ancestors more times than I can count."

CHAPTER 5

Christy hurried down the path to keep up with Cory, who was moving along at almost a full run. She was used to him being extremely confident, and the emotional cracking in his voice had surprised her, as had the obvious fear he seemed to have of his mother. Over the years, she'd seen Mrs. Peters yelling at Cory—usually to watch over Brad and quit teasing him. Christy had come to accept it as part of that family's way; she hadn't considered that was affecting Cory to such a noticeable extent. No such fear of her own mom would have ever motivated or scared Christy in the same way.

As she tried to push the pang of empathy as far away as possible, the reality of the situation hit her full force: Brad and Danny were gone.

On the dock Christy hurried up to Cory, who was already waiting on the end. He'd been here before and knew where to stand just as well as Christy did. They had to shout to be heard above the wind and rain.

"Do you think we're in time?" he asked, the vibration of the dock alerting him to Christy's presence.

"I don't know," she yelled. "The storm is still going strong. Hopefully lightning will strike again before it's over. How long ago did you see them jump?"

Cory pulled out his cell phone, glanced at it quickly, and stashed it back in his pocket. "Almost twenty-five minutes ago."

A few moments later, the sky lit up again and the dock shook from a loud thunderclap.

"That's a good sign. We need to put on our noise protection," Christy shouted. Cory just nodded, never taking his attention from the surface of the pond.

Danny was willing to just sit there catching his breath for as long as Brad was able to hold still and not do anything unexpected.

"Can we wait here for Cory?" Brad asked.

Brad wasn't looking at Danny's face, so he signed "Yes."

Eventually they were going to have to head to the working portal, but if Cory really was planning on

45

coming, they might as well wait around for a few days at Jack's.

Danny propped his pack behind his head and attempted to rest a while. When he was just starting to nod off, Brad's stirring woke him. He had stood up and was walking off towards the bend in the tunnel.

Danny stopped breathing when he noticed an ancient coming towards them from the same bend. It wasn't the Orator or one of the friendly ancients he remembered.

"Brad, no! Come back." Danny jumped up and took three quick steps to catch up with Brad, who was staring at the glistening walls of the cave and tugged hard on his sleeve. He tried to run, tried to pull Brad away with him, but Brad stood there ignoring his pleas. Eventually realizing that it was a futile effort, he gave up, dejected. They had only been in the Empty World for a few minutes and already they were in trouble.

The ancient approached them with his spear pointed at the helpless humans. Brad seemed fascinated by his appearance, ignoring the dangerous-looking spear he wielded. His elongated face looked more horse-like than human, and his stocky upper body, supported by short, equally stocky legs, made for a shocking sight when you first encountered it. Danny had gotten used to it the year before—all but how their eyes moved. Their eyes were set way back on either side of their elongated faces. To look forward, their eyes moved in their sockets in an almost comical way. But this ancient had only one eye. The other socket was hollow, or at least it went so deep that Danny couldn't see anything but blackness.

At the moment though, all Danny could really focus on was that spear. The ancients' spears were the reason for his nightmares that past year. Right now, he and Brad weren't being threatened with it, but it still made him sick to see after having one thrust at him.

Danny was pretty certain that Brad was watching the good eye of their captor as it rotated back and forth, taking them both in. Danny hadn't met this ancient before. He didn't know if that was a good thing or an ominous one. As their captor prodded them deeper into the tunnel, Danny was only relieved that this ancient wasn't Angry Ancient.

They walked prodded onward by their ancient captor for only a few minutes when Danny saw a group of three ancients up ahead. His captor called to the group, and one of them stepped out, setting himself apart. Danny almost screamed. His relief had been short lived. Thirty more steps and Danny was going to be face to face with Angry Ancient.

Clacker was waiting. For what, he wasn't sure. He was inside his human friend Jack's home. Ever since Jack had sought him out asking for the way to the Orator those many cycles ago, he had been uneasy about Jack and his young companions' fates. But strange things were happening; shortly after that meeting with Jack, the Orator himself had come to him and asked for his help. Imagine: an ancient conversing civilly with him! He had never experienced that before.

Clacker had learned that Jack and his companions had found the Orator, but after giving them directions to a rumored portal, the Orator had not seen or heard from Jack again.

Clacker and the Orator had their friendship with Jack in common and the Orator's concern for Jack's whereabouts was why Clacker was here. He had no other ideas or plan, so if waiting was his only plan, this was the place to do it. Eventually, if it was possible, Jack would return here.

Clacker knew that the Orator had gone on to trace Jack's steps to the rumored working portal. At least that's what the Orator had told him he was going to do, and Clacker had no reason to doubt him—beyond the fact, of course, that the Orator was an ancient and they had sworn to eliminate all of Clacker's species for untold decades.

Clacker held no animosity towards the ancients, but they hated him and called the members of his species Cleaners. The term was a derogatory reference to long ago tales of conquest and genocide by Clacker's ancestors, who supposedly appeared in the sky from another world. It was curious, though; for as far back as Clacker's oral traditions went, this world was the only home that either species had ever inhabited. Despite the hatred displayed by all the other ancients, the Orator seemed friendly, even calling him the name that Jack had given him: Clacker.

Another storm was lighting up the failed portal in Jack's tunnel and Clacker decided to head towards the barren portal area outside in hopes that someone from Jack's world might arrive in search of Jack or any of Jack's three companions. Clacker didn't know what had become of Jack or those companions.

Until he knew something definite, he would stay and venture out into the deadly wind when a storm was passing to see if anyone showed up. Without his protective clothing and the animal fat he lathered all over his body, he would surely die by drying out in the fierce wind.

As he headed towards the end of the tunnel where an old portal area lay barren, his senses picked up vibrations that weren't from the storm. He stopped walking and let the vibrations sort themselves out from his feet up a relay system to his brain. They were certainly creature vibrations, but disturbing ones. Some were ancients and some were not. These other vibrations felt as if they were from small forms. Clacker had met many of Jack's species over his cycles, but only three—the young companions of Jack's— who were not mature individuals. He couldn't be sure, but he did not think these vibrations were of the Orator's species. No, there were subtle differences in gait, and therefore the vibration of their strides; these vibrations were almost certainly Jack's species.

He quickened his pace, hoping to catch up to whoever was up ahead. Whatever had brought these young humans and ancients together, it did not bode well.

Danny tried to hide behind Brad and their captor, but it was impossible. As soon as Angry Ancient saw him, his eyes went wide then narrowed, and a vicious grin spread across his face. The second that the two groups converged, Angry Ancient lunged at Danny and backhanded him hard on the side of his head. Danny went down, crying out involuntarily.

He looked up from the floor just as Angry Ancient's mouth started moving. Angry Ancient pointed at one of his charges, an ancient with a beard, the first beard Danny had seen an ancient sporting. The bearded ancient responded by reaching down with grubby hands and roughly pulling Danny up onto his feet.

Angry Ancient turned and looked directly at Brad. The cruel ancient's mouth was still moving rapidly. Brad just stood there, having reverted to his usual timid demeanor with his eyes downcast. Danny watched, concerned that Brad's lack of response would bring on an even angrier reaction than he'd just endured. Danny was never so frustrated that he couldn't read their speech as he was at that moment, when it could have such dire consequences for Brad. After a series of gestures and more rapid mouth movements and a complete lack of response by Brad, Angry Ancient narrowed his eyes, and addressed One-Eyed Ancient. One-Eye's obvious delight in whatever Angry Ancient said, and the short flexible wooden rod he handed to Angry Ancient did not bode well for Brad, Danny was certain.

Angry Ancient took the rod and stepped close to Brad. He mouthed something and prodded Brad with the rod. Brad never looked up or made any indication that he'd heard the ancient or had been bothered in any way by the prodding.

Danny wanted to say something to Brad but the recent memory of the brutal slap, kept him silent. As his worries quickly grew, he smelled something intense, a combination of rotten fish and sour milk—Clacker's protective, and foul-smelling grease. Clacker was somewhere close, and since the smell was getting stronger, Danny deduced that he was getting closer.

Angry Ancient lifted the rod up to strike Brad who still was staring at his own feet, unaware of his danger. Danny's fear for Brad overcame his own and he knew he had to protect Brad and maybe give his unseen friend a warning of the danger he was coming towards. He lunged and shoved Angry Ancient just as Clacker stepped into view waving a spear as intimidating as the ones the ancients carried.

Danny's bold shove and the appearance of Clacker caused a moment of confusion amongst the ancients. Angry Ancient stumbled against the sheer wall for only a second, but it was enough to stop the blow to Brad. Instead, Angry Ancient used his free hand to grab Danny and throw him back, right into Bearded Ancient. Dirty hands reached around and clutched Danny, stopping him from falling but putting him in the spot where he couldn't do anything else. He was held tight.

As he sensed Clacker's slow approached, all Danny could do was watch and struggle against the iron grip of the ancient holding him. Danny knew the Cleaner had seen what just happened. Clacker stopped ten feet or so from Angry Ancient, who was the closest to him, and the Cleaner crouched down, his segmented legs spreading wide as he began to whirl his spear over his head.

Angry Ancient looked like he was accepting the challenge. He too crouched and spread his feet as he dropped the short wooden rod and withdrew his spear that had been strapped to his back. He pointed it straight at Clacker. Bearded Ancient let go of Danny with his right hand and cuffed him on the side of the head. Danny stopped struggling. He couldn't get free anyway so why risk another painful blow to the head? One-Eye was holding onto Brad's arm. They were all watching Angry Ancient and Clacker. Even Brad watched the confrontation.

Angry Ancient was rocking on the balls of his feet, swaying back and forth. Clacker just stood opposite him, twirling his spear menacingly. Nobody else moved until Angry Ancient turned his head away from Clacker. His mouth moved as he glanced at his companions for a second before resuming his stare-down. Whatever he said got the two ancients who were not holding Danny to react. One-Eye released Brad and drew his spear. He and his companion both stepped forward to join Angry Ancient. Only Bearded Ancient didn't move or lessen his grip on Danny.

The situation had become critical. Clacker was outnumbered three to one. Danny felt helpless until Bearded Ancient shifted his stance and his grip slid up closer to Danny's neck. Danny looked down at the three fingers of the ancient's hand. They were stained greenish, dirt or worse in the creases and something black under his cracked nails. Danny closed his eyes against the sight and bit down hard. He tasted grit and something slimy before the ancient reacted to the pain by trying to shake him off. It was the break Danny was looking for. He squirmed free and bolted towards Clacker, sidestepping the startled ancients.

Danny stopped halfway between Clacker and the ancients, holding his arms outstretched, palms out— one towards Clacker, the other towards the ancients. "No, stop! Don't kill him."

Nobody but Brad could understand a word he was saying, but his stance and tone were clear. Angry Ancient separated himself from his companions, dropped his spear, and reached into a side pack dangling from his waist. From it, he withdrew what looked like a horn made of polished yellow metal. He held it by a handle along its side and showed it high in the air. The ancient then pointed the larger end at Clacker and rested his other hand on the small end. Clacker stopped his menacing spear twirling, straightened up, and dropped his spear. Whatever its inherent threat was, the horn had stopped Clacker in his tracks.

Angry Ancient was the first to approach Danny. He hit him again with a powerful swipe of his open hand. This time Danny flew off his feet and crumpled to the floor, out cold.

He didn't know how long he was out for, but when he woke up his face hurt all over and he had trouble focusing his eyes. The first thing that came into sharp focus was the malicious grinning face of Angry Ancient. The ancient bent down and grabbed Danny roughly by the chin, turning his face back and forth. Mouthing something over his shoulder at the other ancients, Angry Ancient used his strength to lift Danny up by his jaw, ignoring his sharp cries of pain.

When the ancient released him and moved away, Danny looked tentatively around for Brad. He finally found him crouched down behind Clacker, who was bound standing up, unable to move. Danny knelt down next to Brad. "You ok?" he asked. "Did anyone hurt you?"

Brad didn't respond so Danny risked tapping him on the knee. Brad shied away but turned his eyes up and signed, "Why did he hit you? Is he going to hit me?"

"He doesn't like me. If you stay out of his way, maybe he'll leave you alone."

Just then Bearded Ancient and a third one, the shortest and foulest smelling adult ancient Danny had ever encountered, came over and roughly pulled both Danny and Brad to their feet. Angry Ancient came over and clapped his hands together. He must have been calling for attention because all the other ancients stopped what they were doing and faced their leader.

Angry Ancient gestured at his crew with his back toward Danny and Brad, occasionally turning to point directly at them. Bearded Ancient gestured angrily and turned away, ignoring anything else that Angry Ancient was saying.

When Angry Ancient stopped talking, Bearded Ancient turned back around and leveled his spear at the two boys. One-Eye and Smelly Ancient did the same. To Danny's surprise, Angry Ancient stepped in and by his demeanor seemed to be defending them.

He addressed each of the ancients in turn, pointed at Clacker and swept his arms in an all-encompassing motion at his companions. The others all dropped their eyes and their spears one by one— the confrontation was over.

Before they had any time to process what had happened, they were handed their ear protectors and their packs, and Clacker's leg bindings were loosened enough for him to walk. When Smelly gave him a rough push, it was clear that they were on the move. But to where or why, Danny had no idea.

CHAPTER 6

The rain was coming at them sideways. Christy waited with Cory while the storm lashed cold water and wind into every nook and cranny of her being. Her ear protectors were the worst. Despite their complete obstruction of all sound, she could still feel the rain pooling inside the pads, creeping into her ears.

In her haste to leave the house, she had only had time to put cloth slippers on, and as her feet began to get numb from the wet and cold, she realized what a big mistake that had been. Regardless, she didn't want to risk soaking everything in her pack by opening it to get her good hiking boots out. She glanced at Cory, and he didn't look any happier than she felt. Every few seconds the lightning flooded the scene and made the trees in the distance and the cattails on the shore stand out in stark, whipping contrasts.

Totally isolated from any sound, hearing was the only one of their senses not being assaulted by the storm. Since they were waiting to follow Danny and Brad to the Empty World, Christy couldn't help but think that what they were experiencing was exactly what Danny always experienced. For her, that lack of sound heightened everything else. The lightning seemed brighter, the rain colder, the wind more fierce. Was it the same for Danny? Were the rest of his senses always ramped up in intensity?

At that moment Christy wasn't sure what was worse: thinking about Danny's world of perpetual silence and what that meant for him or focusing on how uncomfortable and frightening it felt to stand there in the raging storm.

Just as she thought the storm was passing and she'd endured the cold rain for nothing, a bolt of lightning shot down. It hit the pond just right and colors began to swirl. The clap of thunder following the lightning strike was lost on their ears, but Christy still felt the shockwave batter the dock.

Christy grabbed Cory by the sleeve. He started to resist but she held on, waiting until the perfect time. The water below had disappeared, dissolving quickly, to be replaced by clouds of colored fog and the promise of the unknown. Tightening her hold on Cory, she jumped. She felt his tense response as he leaped a split second after her and his sleeve slipped out of her grasp.

Christy rolled at impact and immediately stood up, bracing against the wind. Even though it was as dark out there as it had been at home, the sky gave enough light to see by. Up ahead she could see the familiar outcropping as a dark swelling in the landscape. She knew that the opening to the tunnel was right there. She sensed Cory was behind her slightly, but she didn't dare turn into the wind to check without eye protection.

The barren hillside they stood on used to be a portal tunnel, but it had collapsed, Christy recalled her grandfather saying. Now it was exposed to the elements and driving sand particles were a constant presence from that vantage point. Sand stung every exposed inch of her neck and hands. That's what I get, she thought, hunching her shoulders to push her collar up over her neck as well as she could. If she'd had time to dress properly and been able to choose her own time to return, she'd have been better prepared to face this initial challenge, but there was no point in lamenting the current state of events now. She had to get herself and Cory out of there and into the tunnel up ahead.

Reaching back and feeling for him, she grabbed his coat and pulled him up to his feet. She hoped he understood that now was not the time to question anything, even if they could have communicated effectively.

She stepped back to come even with Cory to avoid having to look behind her, then glanced to see that he had his pack in hand. Letting go of his coat, she started at a run for the tunnel opening she knew was right ahead. She hoped Cory took the hint to follow her, because she couldn't look behind to check.

Within a couple of minutes, she burst through the tunnel entrance and turned, waiting. Cory was right behind, and she motioned him forward as she switched on her flashlight and started moving again. She stopped running but kept a fast walking pace until they were much further into the tunnel where the walls brightened, shimmering with a pale bluish green pearly glow. Finally, she stopped and took off her noise protection. Cory followed suit.

"What's in here? Where's that light coming from?" he asked, breathing heavy from the exertion. He was looking around at the smooth walls, taking it all in.

"My grandfather and I haven't figured that out. You'll get used to it soon." She frowned. "I was hoping to find Brad and Danny here. They may be just ahead near the portal chamber."

"Portal? The one that comes out in France?"

Christy shook her head. "That portal is days away. This is the one that stopped working and stranded my grandfather here. Come on, let's get to the chamber. If they're not there, then Danny probably took Brad to my grandfather's place. I hope the drawbridge is down or else we have to turn around and find our way all on the outside to my grandfather's. And I'm not sure I can find it traveling outside the tunnel."

Christy started moving again, following the winding tunnel, and Cory hurried to keep up. The tunnel sloped downward just as she remembered, and Christy knew they were traveling deep inside the hill. It wasn't long before they broke out into the widened cavern with the now useless portal.

Christy didn't stop to see how the strangeness of it all was affecting Cory, because at the moment she wasn't thinking of him or what he must be experiencing. She was still feeling too elated at being back. And because of the circumstances, she'd really had no choice in that matter. She didn't feel guilt for breaking her promise to her parents; this was Cory's fault, not hers.

Fortunately, the bridge was down, but Danny and Brad weren't there as Christy had hoped, so she proceeded on through the tunnel. After crossing the bridge, they started up a slow incline towards the end of the tunnel. When Christy saw darkness ahead she stopped.

"We're coming out into a protected area and we won't need to put our ear protection back on. About a quarter of a mile or so through this area we'll see my grandfather's tunnel. It's dark inside his tunnel so we'll need our flashlights there until we find the torches in his place."

Cory nodded in reply. When they stepped out of the tunnel and into the night, alien sounds and smells hit them. Christy raised her hand to halt them, knowing Cory must have felt overwhelmed by the sights. Even though it was still dark, the strangeness of it all was pressing down on them. Christy had felt almost out of her body when she and Danny came out to this spot with her grandfather for the first time. She let Cory be for a minute as he listened and looked around, eyes wide.

Way off in the distance, carried to them by the wind, a screech kept repeating, rhythmically, over and over. What must have been an answer, or a challenge, echoed a jarring high-pitched screech. In the background were the buzzings of the many different kinds of alien insects.

Low to the ground and very close to where they were standing, little twinkles of light kept flashing on and off—first a light purple, then an intense yellow, back and forth, spread out for what seemed like a dozen yards or so all around them. Too many different sights and sounds bombarded them all at once to make sense of any of it, yet in so many ways it was like back home in the summer as evening turned to night—day creatures relinquishing the stage to be replaced by the night creatures looking for food or mates, all of them announcing their intentions in their own unique ways.

With the decreased wind, the smells were more intense, not scattered as they were in the exposed areas. Although they were familiar now to her, she knew Cory would be trying to make sense of what his nose was telling him.

She watched his face and broke into his confused thoughts when she saw him take in a deep breath.

"Florida … and vanilla, mixed in."

"Huh?" Then he sniffed again. "Never been to Florida but it smells like the butterfly house at the Museum of Science, only a lot nicer." Cory sniffed loudly then said, "Cream soda."

Christy smiled and nodded. She let him be for a few more seconds.

After the short pause, she said, "Okay, we have to get going now. Let's hurry."

"Hurry *now*? What have we been doing?" Cory snorted, unpleasantly.

Christy rolled her eyes and gestured for him to follow. To his credit, he cooperated without another complaint.

Sweeping her flashlight across the ground as they hurried, Christy found the path and the opening to her grandfather's home that he'd lived in for the nine years he'd been stranded. Shining her light into the tunnel, she motioned Cory to follow.

When they arrived at the wide chamber that was her grandfather's home, it became clear that neither he, nor Brad, nor Danny were there. Christy fought her overwhelming disappointment, knowing it would only hinder their progress; they had to keep looking. Everywhere was pitch black except for where their lights were shining. Christy set her pack down and rummaged around in it. Removing a cigarette lighter, she reached up to one of the torches in its receptacle on the wall and lit it, then switched off her flashlight to gauge the effect. Satisfied, she decided not to light any of the dozen or so other torches, which her grandfather had installed around the cave's perimeter.

"My grandfather used flint and steel to light fires, but I don't know anything about that. Danny was good at it though," she said.

"What's flint and steel?" Cory asked. He was looking around at the bit of cave within the limits of the one lit torch.

"I guess you've never been in scouts like Trevor and Danny," Christy said. She thought of how she'd planned the trip with Trevor and then gone without him the first time she came to the Empty World. Feeling bad, she had to give him his due.

"Trevor's the one who gave me most of the list of things to pack. I would have brought matches, but a lighter is so much more practical. It doesn't get wet and fail at the worst time. Without his input, my pack would have been virtually useless, except for the ear protection. I decided to bring them even though I didn't know why they were important at the time."

Cory rolled his eyes and used his flashlight to see further into the depths of the cave.

"Save your batteries," Christy said. "We can just light a couple more torches."

"Who died and left you in charge?" Cory asked.

Christy switched her flashlight on again and directed it right at Cory's eyes.

"Shut that off!" he yelled.

She did reluctantly, then sighed and said, "I guess I should point out that Brad and Danny clearly aren't here. That means we have to go looking for them, and they could be anywhere. We're going to need every ounce of light these flashlights can give us. So shut yours off. Ok?"

Cory stared at her hard for a few seconds before eventually conceding her point and turning his flashlight off.

"So where are they, Walker?"

Christy was thinking quickly, trying to hold off the panic, which the reality of their predicament was beginning to cause. "I can't believe they're not here. We weren't that far behind them. I can't imagine that Danny would head out at night if he were with Brad. I'd have brought him here and waited till morning."

Christy started pacing. "Unless Brad ran ahead. Maybe he panicked when he got here, and Danny couldn't keep up or something."

Christy busied herself by lighting two more torches. The extra light illuminated almost the whole cavern and sparkled off the crystal stacks that her grandfather had collected over the years. Cory walked over to the crystals, intrigued by them, but stopped short and made a face.

"Oh, what's that smell?" he asked.

Christy barely heard him, as preoccupied as she was with worrying. When she realized he had said something, she stopped pacing.

"Huh? What?" Then the foul odor hit her too. Sniffing out where the smell was coming from, she identified its source. It was a plastic bucket full of semi-solid grease.

"I know what this is," she said, trying to decipher the memory that was slowly unscrambling itself. "I've smelled this before, but it wasn't here when I was here with my grandfather."

"What is it?" Cory asked. Christy paused. Finally it hit her.

"It's this stuff that Clacker covers his body with when he goes outside in the wind." Christy looked more closely at the things that were strewn around the chamber. "I think he's been here."

"You mean the insect guy? So what?" Cory said.

"He helped us get home and told us how to find the Orator. Didn't Rob tell you about him?"

"Just his name and what he looked like ... nothing else. Rob wasn't really talking to me when he got back," Cory mumbled.

"I can't understand why not," Christy said sarcastically.

She walked around, picking some things up here and there to inspect them, then said, "I think Clacker hasn't just been here— I think he's staying here, or was. Maybe he's waiting for my grandfather."

"What does it matter? How's he going to help us find Brad and Flying Fingers?"

"Really? You can't think how having someone friendly to us could be a help? If he's staying here, we should wait for him— maybe he has some information about my grandfather or Brad and Danny. And if he's not about to molt like last time I met him, maybe he'll come looking for them with us," she said.

"If Brad was here, it couldn't have been more than a half hour before we got here. Where is he?" Cory asked.

"I don't know, but Clacker might have taken them out of here and be helping them to the portal, if they did come this far," Christy replied, obviously exasperated. "Although, like I said, I can't imagine them leaving here at night."

Christy began pacing again, mentally back where she had started. Suddenly she stopped and turned to Cory.

"Did you know Brad was going to use the portal?" she asked.

"Yeah, well ... uh ..." Cory stumbled over his words, pausing before he continued. "I guess we kind of planned to go together."

Christy had had similar plans, so the admission didn't exactly surprise her, but she still was having trouble wrapping her head around one detail. "So how come he went with Danny then, and not you?"

"He didn't. Flying Fingers followed him, I think. At least from what it looked like. But it's not like it was easy to see or anything. It was dark. I saw the little brat running along the shore when Brad jumped in and then he bolted onto the dock and caught the portal before it closed," Cory explained, then added, "I don't know why Brad went alone. We planned to go together.

But he kept going over what we were planning, over and over, wouldn't quit with it. Every day, nonstop, yap, yap." At that point Cory hesitated and groaned.

"What?" Christy asked.

Cory shook his head. "I— I think Brad went because I threatened to go alone," he replied. "When he gets something in his head, he doesn't let go. He wouldn't drop it, so I told him to shut up about our plans or I'd go alone. I know him though, I should have figured out that would make him do something stupid."

Cory ran his fingers through his hair and took a seat on the nearby cot before he continued. "All my life I've had to be careful about what I say around him because you never know what he's gonna do. Sometimes my mom even says or does something that Brad screws up in his mind and reacts to all weird. She says it's his ...ah, what do you call it—"

"Asperger's," Christy filled in.

"Yeah, that's it," Cory said. "When I was making my plan to run away through the portal, the thought of being somewhere without him was what kept me going. You have no idea what it's like at home."

Christy was surprised at Cory's honesty. "He's always seemed ok to me," she said, "other than not looking anyone in the eye, always looking at the ground. And he's amazing at learning things like when we meet with Danny to learn sign language. He puts the rest of us to shame."

"Oh, yeah," Cory replied, bitterly. "Try spending twenty-four seven with him and my mom like I do."

Cory then rested his elbows on his knees and buried his face in his arms.

Christy didn't know how to respond, so she changed the subject. "I think we should try to get some sleep and wait till daylight to decide what to do or where to look for them. I'm tired. Maybe in the meantime Clacker or Brad and Danny will show up."

Cory lifted his head up and nodded, clearly just as tired as she was. And since Christy knew Cory had very limited knowledge of the Empty World, she really didn't expect him to object.

CHAPTER 7

Danny and Brad were being forced to march without stopping. The dawn was just breaking, and they'd been walking for a couple of hours already. Since Angry Ancient's hands and mouth were in constant motion, Danny quickly realized that Angry Ancient was the group's leader.

Despite his growing fatigue and fear, Danny noticed that Angry Ancient had not once used sign language as his companions occasionally did; he relied only on exaggerated pantomimes to get his point across. Danny wondered why this was— he had seen the ancient use sign language before—but he didn't think about it too much. His focus was more on his concern for Brad.

Brad had been stumbling off and on for the better part of the long march to their mystery destination. At one point, when Brad staggered off the trail they were on and collapsed, Angry Ancient stood over him, obviously seething with anger. Danny was surprised by the restraint he showed— he didn't lash out and hurt or even touch the clearly exhausted boy.

The ancient simply pointed at two of his companions to do it for him. One of them stepped over to Brad and hit him with a backhand across the face, while the other grabbed him under his arms and lifted him up, supporting him as they continued on. Watching them treat Brad so roughly made Danny feel ill. He was concerned for him, but with one of the ancients walking behind him, occasionally prodding him with his spear, Danny could only steal worried glances at Brad for seconds at a time. The one time that Angry Ancient caught him looking towards Brad, he cuffed Danny across the back of his head, making him stumble too. With all the ancients taking orders from Angry Ancient, there wasn't one of them that Danny would have labeled Protector Ancient.

Several hours after they had started walking, they came to a hill and stopped. Danny hadn't seen this particular hill before, but it was similar to the other outcroppings, most of which seemed to have tunnels within them. When the ancients began removing their heavy packs, it became clear that this was going to be a stopping point.

The break came not a second too soon for one of the ancients who had been helping Brad walk. The ancient had given up trying to pull Brad by the arms and had hefted him across his broad shoulders; now he just let Brad slip out of his arms and onto the hard-packed trail, not seeming to care that it was a drop of several feet.

Brad curled up into a ball. Sensing that the ancients were temporarily preoccupied, Danny sat down next to Brad and tapped him on the shoe, hoping he would take it as a sign of support. He was about to start signing with Brad when Angry Ancient looked over and gestured threateningly, so Danny discarded any thoughts of communicating with his friend and just watched the activity around him.

Smelly Ancient pulled from his pack a large, flat, square piece of metal that glistened in the reddish daylight. In a quick second, the ancient ran his hand along one of the edges and the metal separated into several layers. Then he locked the corners together and produced what Danny thought looked very much like a reflector oven he'd seen some of the older Boy Scouts in his troop using. But there was no way this could be used like one of those reflector ovens. The fierce wind would never allow a fire started outside of this thing to reflect its heat into the shiny inner surfaces. Danny only had to wonder at its purpose for a second before the ancient produced some square pellets and placed them in the middle of the device. He then reached into his pocket and produced a small thick strip of metal, a roundish crystal, and a charred piece of cloth. Within seconds the ancient had produced a spark and a fire was blazing inside the boxy contraption, well protected from the wind. Within minutes, the impromptu fire was the focal point of the ancients, who seemed relieved to be resting.

Bearded Ancient reached into a side pack and produced a creature which Danny had come to refer to as a bowling ball baby. They were harmless marsupials whose only defense seemed to be an ability to curl into a tight little ball, spray slick, glandular oil on the ground ahead of themselves, and roll off away from danger with the help of the fierce wind.

Danny watched in horror as the ancients all prodded the helpless creature with their spears. The little furry animal rolled up and sprayed its oil, trying to escape, but each time it started to roll off, the ancient closest to it prodded it sharply in the opposite direction. All the ancients participated in teasing the poor animal, seemingly delighted by the sport of it. After at least twenty minutes of watching the creature spray and roll only to be tormented and prodded in the opposite direction, back and forth, back and forth, as if it were an inanimate object for them to play with, one of the ancients seemed to grow bored and impaled the creature with his spear, holding it up high to squirm until it finally stopped moving. Danny turned away, disgusted by the spectacle.

To his added horror, the ancients didn't even cook the creature. They just flung it off into the strange tan-colored moss lining the trail. After cooking up something else rummaged from out of their packs, they packed up and walked through the meandering tunnel for another hour before stopping. Angry Ancient took his ear plugs out, which prompted the others to do the same, and One-Eye and Bearded Ancient slid down to the tunnel floor to rest. After saying something, Angry Ancient walked off deeper into the tunnel. Danny noticed the other ancients seemed to relax as soon as Angry Ancient was out of sight. He watched their faces when they spoke, and Danny was pretty sure that some of them were even laughing because the corners of their mouths turned up.

Danny turned to Brad who was leaning against the tunnel wall. His eyes were red from crying.

"Are you alright, Brad?" he whispered. He was surprised when Brad nodded almost immediately. Danny looked again at the ancients to make sure none of them had a problem with him speaking. One-Eye Ancient was looking his way but didn't seem especially interested. Danny was about to say something else when Brad spoke and signed.

"Cory won't be able to find us here."

"No, Brad, I think you're right. He won't," Danny replied softly.

Just then, Clacker, who had been standing apart as Shorty Ancient held a spear to his midsection, made a series of movements. Danny could tell Clacker was also talking because he could see the Cleaner's slit of a mouth moving. Christy had described to Danny how

Clacker's language sounded like the clicking castanets of Flamenco dancers. Danny couldn't remember if he'd ever heard castanets before he lost his hearing, so he could only imagine what they actually sounded like.

When Danny looked towards Clacker, the Cleaner lifted his left front pincher and tapped his bullet-shaped head with it, extending the pincher out again in a decent approximation of the sign for hello. Danny smiled and responded, just as he'd done when they'd first met. Ignoring the spear pointed at him, Clacker bowed slightly at the waist, and Shorty Ancient seemed unperturbed.

Danny watched as Clacker gave the sign for Jack with his crude sign language, which was hampered by his pincher hands. Then he signed Danny's name too.

Danny replied by simplifying his signing as he'd done the year before. "Do you know where Jack is?"

No signing was needed as Clacker shook his head no.

Danny sighed. There was nothing he could think to say in response. Out of the corner of his eye, Danny saw Brad opening his mouth and contorting it in an odd way. He couldn't imagine what sounds Brad was making, and attempting to read his lips left him without any clues.

Whatever Brad was doing, Clacker appeared to be responding to it, and Danny watched as the two of them went back and forth apparently communicating. With each back and forth response, Brad twisted his mouth oddly. Danny thought it looked almost as if Brad were attempting to spit, as his lips vibrated rapidly, and his chest heaved, expanding and contracting as rapidly as he flapped his lips.

For nearly ten minutes, Danny watched fascinated. Finally, he just couldn't contain himself. He grabbed Brad by the arm to get his attention. "Are you two talking?" he signed.

Brad nodded and turned back to Clacker. Danny couldn't believe it. He watched for a few minutes more then got Brad's attention again. "Christy says Clacker's language sounds like just a series of clicks. Do you understand it?"

Brad shook his head no. He signed, "Not yet. He's teaching me."

"Are you imitating his language?" Danny asked.

Brad nodded, and signed, "I think I almost have the sounds right, all but one that I can't do yet."

Danny was amazed. Even after knowing Brad for almost a year, he was still getting used to Brad's literal way of answering questions, and his sometimes-uncanny learning abilities. Despite his 'not yet' response, in less than fifteen minutes, it appeared that Brad was on his way to learning Clacker's language. Danny did know it was possible since the Orator had told them that he'd learned the Cleaner's language, but Jack had been stranded here for years and didn't understand anything Clacker said. The two of them had had to use the modified sign language to talk.

Danny wanted to watch and ask more questions but, that chance was taken away from him. Angry Ancient returned and soon they were on the move again. To where, Danny didn't know. He suspected they were probably heading to Angry Ancient's village that was within a day's walk of the glider clearing. If that was where they were going, then they were headed where Danny would have taken Brad anyway. Except now they were prisoners.

Christy woke up cramped and still tired. Her grandfather's cots weren't as comfortable as she remembered.

She switched on a flashlight and quickly lit the torches to brighten the cavern. Then she walked over to the still sleeping Cory and shook him by the shoulder. He twisted in his sleep and pulled away from Christy's hand. She tried again only to be slapped away.

"Get up," she whined. "This isn't home, you can't sleep all morning."

Cory just continued to ignore her. She waited for a minute and when he didn't budge, she placed her foot on the small of his back and pushed. The force of her foot rocked the cot as Cory's body shifted to the edge. Both the cot and Cory ended up twisted on the floor. Christy walked away. "I'm leaving in half an hour," she shouted. "If you want to tag along, you'd better get off the floor. Oh, and I know where all the edible stuff that we have to live off of on our trip is, so unless you want to go by yourself and starve on the way, let's go."

"Hey! What'd you do that for?" Cory yelled. "I was getting up."

"Not fast enough," Christy replied. Cory was picking himself off the floor. She grabbed one of the dozen empty milk crates that her grandfather had brought from earth and sat down on it.

"My grandfather laid down the law," she said. "Before we left here for Clacker's place, he said that when he told us to do something we were to do it immediately, because our lives depended on it. You get the same order. You do what I say, no questions asked."

"Not a chance, Walker," Cory said as he stood up and loomed over her.

"Listen Cory, Brad and Danny aren't here, and I don't think waiting around will change that. Danny knows where this is. He'd have brought Brad here if he could. Or we'd have seen them in that first tunnel as soon as we came through the portal. Since that didn't happen, we have to go looking for them. No matter what, all of us eventually need to get to the working portal. Danny knows the way there just as well as I do, so that's where we're heading." She got up and stood nose to nose with Cory. "Do you know how to get to the portal?" she asked.

Cory pushed Christy out of his face. "I'm not taking orders from you. Just because I need you to get to the working portal, doesn't mean you're in charge. If it wasn't for you starting this whole thing, we wouldn't be in this mess."

"Me?" Christy was incredulous. "If you hadn't lied to Brad, or teased him, he wouldn't be missing, and we wouldn't be trying to find him. This is your fault."

Cory took a deep breath and nodded, surprising Christy. "Yeah, I did that. But you can't blame me for Brad's screwed up thought process. This all goes right back to you. You're to blame, Walker, and you know it." Cory started to move past Christy, but she grabbed him as he stepped by her.

"Wait, Cory," she said quietly, trying to defuse the rising argument.

He shook her off but turned around, waiting.

"Yes, I started this whole thing. My mistake was letting you see me standing on the dock that night, but you were the one who pushed Rob in or none of us would have ever come here."

When Cory didn't react right away, she continued. "Listen, we have to do this together. I don't want to boss you around, but you can't always want to do just the opposite of what I say. I've been here before, and you haven't. That's just the way it is."

Cory stared. "Walker, you're right," he snarled. "I need you, but I don't like you, or the situation."

"News flash, I don't like you either."

"Good!" Cory yelled.

"Good!" Christy screamed back, and both their voices echoed off the steep walls into the distance.

As the echoes faded, the chamber became all the more silent in contrast. After a few minutes, Christy had calmed down. "We should hurry to eat," she said. "You do have something to eat in your pack, right?"

Cory stammered for a second then replied, "Yeah, of course, I have food. Pretzels, mostly."

"Pretzels? That's it?" She shook her head. "You're lucky that my grandfather has all these sealed jars with dried fruits. I even think he has beef jerky." She frowned. "Well, I'm not sure what kind of meat it is, but it's dried and sealed tight so it shouldn't be spoiled. You're lucky. You'd starve without it. You have to be prepared, Trevor always says."

"You know, Walker, you could be nicer about this. As you so happily pointed out, I'm not in scouts. I did the best I could."

Christy sighed. The constant competition between them had gotten the better of her, it seemed. She supposed if she hadn't had Trevor's help the first time, she'd have been just as unprepared. Thought she couldn't imagine only bringing pretzels. "Sorry," Christy said. "I know. I was just kidding about letting you starve. You know that, I hope."

"Oh, I don't know. I think you might enjoy watching me starve," Cory said, a smile reluctantly appearing on his face. Christy smiled back.

"What if your grandfather hasn't been back in a year? None of that stuff will be good still, will it?" Cory sounded afraid.

She shook her head. "It will be fine. The containers are all airtight. They can last a long time like that."

Cory started to open some of the food jars and began stuffing dried fruit and whatever else he could find into his pack.

"Cory, not like that! You need to pack it in plastic bags. Or take only the stuff from home that's sealed in the foil. The bags are over there on that shelf." She pointed. "If you don't put the loose stuff in the bags and it gets hot on the trip to the working portal, the moisture in the air and the heat will make the fruit and meat spoil." She pointed to another shelf against the back of the cavern. "That's where he keeps the bottles of water. I can't imagine they would be bad. We won't have to take more than a few small bottles of water with us—just enough for today. It would be too heavy otherwise, and there is plenty of fresh, drinkable water on the way."

At the mention of water, Cory looked uncomfortable, shifting his weight from one foot to the other.

Christy pointed. "Around that bend," she said. Then she grinned as Cory hurried off. She wasn't sure, but she thought she heard a mumbled thank you.

CHAPTER 8

Connie Walker knocked on Christy's bedroom door. Her daughter hadn't come downstairs that morning, which was unusual. She was usually always up early.

"Christy, you up yet?" Connie waited for a response. When she got none, she gently opened the door and looked in. Christy wasn't in her bed, and her bed hadn't been made. The bathroom was also empty.

Why would she have headed to Trevor's this early? Mrs. Walker wondered. Trevor was not the earliest of risers— possibly Ginny's then. She took her phone out and was about to call Ginny's mom when she stopped, remembering the violent thunderstorm the night before. A queasy tightening took hold of her stomach. The phone vibrated in her hand, startling her momentarily.

"Hello?"

"Connie?"

"Yes."

"This is Abigail Peters."

A call from Abigail was strange— perhaps not as strange as it would have been before the events of last year, but still a rare thing.

"What can I do for you, Abigail?" Connie asked distractedly, a growing concern for Christy making the question come out as disingenuous.

"Are the boys over there? Both of them aren't here and they haven't left a note. And it's so early. Cory's never up this early. Brad never leaves the house without telling me." Abigail was rambling. Her fear was palpable.

Hearing that tone in Abigail's voice made the tightening in Connie's stomach worse.

"Did you see them at all this morning?" Connie asked, fearing the answer.

"No. When Brad didn't come out for breakfast, I peeked into their room and their beds looked slept in, but they were gone. And ... they took their packs."

"What packs?" Connie asked, now really beginning to worry.

"Both the boys had backpacks under their beds. I, I don't know what they had in them but I kind of liked that the two of them were doing something, planning something together."

"Abigail!" Connie admonished.

"What?"

"What were they planning?" Connie asked.

"I don't know. You know children. They're always dreaming up things," Abigail said offhandedly.

"Abigail, they're not little children anymore. They're fourteen. And when fourteen-year-olds plan things in secret, it's not usually about captaining a pirate ship or running away to join the circus."

Abigail was silent for a moment. "I know, really I do. I guess I hoped they were just getting along better. But I'm worried."

Just then Connie's phone beeped, signaling another call.

"Abigail, I'll call you right back. I have another call," Connie said and pressed to answer the new call.

"Hello?"

"Connie? This is Katie Lake. Have you seen Danny? He wasn't in his bed this morning when I looked in."

Connie was reeling. She was afraid she knew the answer to where the kids were.

"Katie," she began, "I think we have a serious problem."

Danny walked beside Brad, mile after mile. The more they walked, the less interest the ancients seemed to have in them. As long as they were under guard by at least one of them, the rest, including Angry Ancient, ignored them. Whenever they entered a protected area and could take off their ear protection, Danny watched fascinated as Brad and Clacker continued their conversations.

Darkness was falling when they finally stopped for good for the night behind a huge stand of intertwined trees— over generations the trees had adapted to the strong wind by wrapping their narrow branches through their neighbor's to stand tall in a shared act of defiance. The sound of the wind was just a mildly annoying, whining pitch in the background.

Danny was preparing a spot to sleep and was ignoring the screaming pain in his legs. Brad was clearly exhausted as well. Danny tapped him on the shoulder and Brad flinched, bothered by the touch.

"Brad," Danny signed, "I'll scoop out a spot for you to sleep."

Brad stared at his own feet but signed back, "Cory will not be able to find us here."

Danny had expected something like that. He tapped Brad on his foot for attention and received just a slight pulling away, not the exaggerated recoil he received when he tried to touch him on his arm or shoulder.

"Brad, you have to start realizing that Cory may not be coming at all. As soon as my mom and your mom find out that we're missing, they'll figure out what happened and then Cory will never get the chance to follow you. And even if he did manage to make it here, he has no idea where we are or even how to get to the working portal. You do know that we are prisoners of these aliens, right?"

"Why?" Brad signed.

Danny shook his head. "I don't know why they took us prisoner. And I don't know where we're going, although I can take a guess."

Brad showed no reaction. "Clacker says we're leaving, that's why Cory won't find us here," he signed. "I need Cory to find us."

Danny was surprised at that response. He wasn't sure what Brad meant.

"What do you mean we're leaving?" he signed. "Tell me what Clacker meant." Danny was searching for how to ask Brad to get the most information from him. "Tell me exactly what Clacker said to you."

Brad stared back at his own feet and signed, "Clacker said that tonight when we stop, he will help us escape."

"You mean from here? Now? This is where we've stopped for the night. What else did he say?"

"He said to tell you to be ready. He is going to ..."

Brad seemed to be searching for a word—he spelled "incapacitate" then continued to sign, "the ancients and then lead us away from here."

"How is he going to do that?" Danny asked, his hands flying.

Brad didn't answer; he just put his hands on the side of his temples and appeared to be squeezing his head. Danny tried to pull Brad's hands away. Brad reacted badly, almost falling backwards as he tried to escape Danny's touch, but kept his hands by his side. Danny repeated his signing.

Brad seemed at first to ignore Danny but then he signed, "I don't know, but I need to put my ear protection on when Clacker signals me. He said you don't need to."

Danny nodded, hoping he understood.

They were given water and something to eat by Smelly Ancient, who pointed towards the spots Danny had prepared for the two of them. It was a clear sign that they were settling down for the night. The ancients ignored Clacker, who stood apart a bit, occupying the space they had allotted for him. Clacker's jet-black eyes stayed focused on Brad and Danny till the ancients snuffed out their torches and settled down.

Danny remained alert, crawling close to Brad once they couldn't be seen in the dark. The night was the blackest he'd ever seen. This world didn't have a moon, and the sky was overcast with no stars at all. He had to wait what seemed like forever before he finally felt Brad stirring. Then Brad stood up, pulling at Danny as he did. All Danny could do was follow Brad's lead.

Suddenly a dark shadow loomed over them, barely discernible in the coal black night. He felt one of Clacker's pinchers on his arm, pulling him. Brad stumbled against him, almost knocking him off balance. At least he hoped it was Brad. In the darkness, he let himself be led, sometimes nearly dragged at a run, trusting Clacker. Without any light and without sound, what other options did he have?

Christy was in the lead. They were going too slow and she didn't like it. As of yet, without being able to communicate, she hadn't been able to impress upon Cory the need for haste. She had tried to pull him along by the sleeve, but he had shaken her off numerous times and followed at his own pace, forcing her to slow down or lose him. Finally, they hit a stretch protected from the sound and she motioned Cory to take off his ear protection as she did the same.

"You are the slowest thing on two legs," she screamed at him. "Oh boy, you must be out of shape."

"What?" he asked, throwing his hands up.

"What did you think I kept pulling your sleeve for?" Christy replied. "Now that we can talk for a bit, I'm letting you know that I'm going at my pace and you have to keep up, or else."

"Or else what, Walker?"

"Or else, you'll be trying to find your way on your own. Don't forget it. Keep up." Christy started off, but Cory yelled after her.

"Hey, can't we rest a few minutes? Come on," he pleaded. She turned.

"This was the rest," she yelled, and kept right on going.

She only waited a minute or two before glancing behind her. Cory was keeping up step for step, although he pouted the whole time. At least his deep gulps for air as they pushed on kept him from complaining.

Christy led for another thirty minutes until the spongy moss underfoot finally began to take its toll on her. She pulled up and stopped behind a small grouping of plants that had made it to about head height before they seemed to give up, bunch together, and fold over on themselves. Christy suspected it was their way of surviving the constant wind. She slipped her backpack off gratefully and slid down, resting against the plants and taking advantage of the slight protection they offered.

Cory took his cue from her and slid his own pack off. He sat down beside her. "Does this wind ever stop?" he asked. He was still visibly breathing heavily.

Christy really just wanted to rest without talking but she responded reluctantly. "No, it only gets a little less in areas. To really get out of the wind we have to get into one of the tunnels or to the backside of one of the larger outcroppings."

Cory huffed, still calming down from their tough walk through the moss.

"You're unbelievable," Christy remarked. "You don't know squat about this world and yet you and Brad planned to come here. Why?"

Cory was silent. As if to answer her, he reached into his pack and took out a very expensive looking digital camera, complete with a long telephoto lens. The whole thing must have weighed several pounds.

Christy shook her head in amazement. "You guys wanted to risk your lives to take pictures? You're really something, you know that."

Cory leaned forward. "Who are you to judge me?" he asked. "Brad and I want to document this world.

What's wrong with that? I could care less about keeping this place secret."

Christy leaned forward too, poking her finger into Cory's chest. "As long as you're with me, you won't use that camera. Got it? If you do, I'll find a way to leave you in the dust or steal that thing and throw it away while you're sleeping. Don't think I won't."

Cory leaned back but locked eyes with Christy. Finally, he shrugged and closed his eyes. Christy waited but Cory stayed silent, so she closed her eyes too, grateful for a few quiet minutes.

When Christy opened her eyes again, she was disoriented, realizing she had dozed off. The day was fast coming to an end— the light fading with the setting red-tinged sun. The ground around her was almost purple with the deep shadows of evening. She must have slept for hours.

She turned to say something to Cory, but nobody was there. Cory was gone, backpack and all.

CHAPTER 9

They were moving slowly now after the initial rush. Being led through the dark after their escape, Danny only had one of Clacker's pinchers for guidance. Occasionally Clacker tugged harder and they picked up their pace again—though Danny couldn't discern any rhyme or reason for why they varied their speed. Terrain didn't seem to be a deciding factor since it hadn't yet varied from the spongy moss and level ground they were traveling through. Danny didn't usually feel handicapped by his deafness, but with his sight gone too, he was completely dependent on the strong, almost painful grasp of Clacker's pincher, and until told otherwise, he didn't dare reach for a flashlight.

Thinking of his flashlight, it suddenly dawned on him that he didn't have his backpack. How could he have not made sure he had it in his grasp before they started! He had been too focused on Brad and Clacker interacting, he thought. Now he was in trouble. Even if they made it away successfully, being without his pack could still spell trouble going forward, but at the moment he had to let the thought go. There was no going back for it now.

After some minutes alternating between a slow walk and a brisk stride, Clacker picked up his pace even more— quicker and quicker— almost to a sprint. Danny couldn't imagine how Clacker was seeing well enough to go so fast without one of them stumbling into something or tripping. Maybe Clacker could see in the dark better than he or Brad could. He hoped that was the case.

Brad stepped on one of Danny's feet several times in the next twenty minutes, almost sending the both of them sprawling to the ground. Without Clacker's steadying grasp, he and Brad would have tripped more than once. When they finally got to a stretch of particularly spongy moss that slowed them down and sapped their energy, Clacker let go of Danny and they stopped.

While resting, Danny still couldn't discern much more than the shapes of his companions. He'd never seen a darker night. With clouds blocking out all starlight, he could barely see his own hands in front of his face.

Startled out of his contemplation, Danny felt Brad's hand on his arm, and then a strap being looped over it. Danny smiled; Brad had given him his backpack. Danny was overwhelmed with relief, and even more impressed by his new friend knowing that he must have been carrying Danny's pack the whole length of their escape from the ancients. That was a lot of running in the dark hefting two backpacks.

Danny thought back to teaching Brad sign language at the Peters' house. Brad was the best at sign language by far, surpassing Christy, Rob, and Trevor, and at the end of a day's lesson, Danny told him so. Mrs. Peters overheard and commented that Brad would surprise them with his determination and the many hidden talents he had that sometimes came out at unexpected moments.

Just in the time since they'd been captured by the ancients, Danny had been the beneficiary of those talents twice— first when Brad learned Clacker's language in record time and conveyed the escape plan, and second when he grabbed Danny's pack in the dark as they carried out that plan.

Danny shouldered his pack as Brad and Clacker huddled around him. Clacker took out a flashlight and handed it to Brad, who turned it on. Danny figured it was a sign that Clacker knew they were in no danger from their former captors, at least for the moment. Danny saw Clacker's mouth moving so he took the flashlight from Brad and trained it on his friend's hands. Brad nodded. "Clacker says we have to keep moving," he signed to Danny. "But we can rest for a minute first."

"How did Clacker incapacitate the ancients?" Danny asked.

He watched as Brad's mouth moved strangely and waited for Clacker to respond. "He said the ancients aren't the only ones with sound that can kill or render others helpless," Brad signed. "Clacker can make a highpitched sound with his mouth that knocks the ancients out. It would have affected me too, but Clacker warned me, and I put on my ear protection. The ancients need their horn device to do the same to Clacker, so he has the advantage as long as the ancients don't realize he has that ability."

Danny nodded. "Where do we go now?" he signed.

Brad turned to speak with Clacker. After Clacker replied, Brad turned to Danny and signed, "Clacker says he thinks the best thing to do is take us to the working portal. He says you must know the way once we get beyond the big swamp."

Danny nodded, and Clacker bowed his head, acknowledging he understood. Then Clacker signed in his crude fashion and spoke aloud, while Brad translated, "I am afraid to bring you by myself. We must find some friends of mine first. With others of my species, I would feel more at ease about our chances." Then he added, "But to find my friends, we must go through the fire that rises from the ground."

Danny felt wary. He didn't know what the statement meant, but it didn't sound promising and it definitely sounded dangerous.

Christy stood up in the waning light and looked around. She felt helpless. The spongy moss hid any footprints that might have helped her determine where Cory went. All she could do was guess where he was. Why he'd left was another matter. She was pretty sure he'd left to do just what she'd warned him not to— take pictures.

Now she faced her first real dilemma since coming back to the Empty World— should she wait there, assuming Cory would come back? It was the smart thing to do if he really was just out taking pictures. It was almost dark now and he'd have to be back soon. But if for some reason he hadn't left to use his camera, where was he? He'd never get to the working portal on his own, she was sure of that. So, should she go looking for him?

Sure, the smart thing was to wait, but Christy had a sick feeling in her stomach that wouldn't go away. She had no idea how long it had been since Cory had taken off. And what if he wasn't out there taking pictures? Or what if he had gone for that and then something had happened?

With conflicting emotions, she made a decision. She picked up her pack and headed out from the small protection of the tightly packed plants. The light was now almost gone, and a high mist was settling in. Watching the mist, she stopped in her tracks for a moment.

That should be impossible, she thought. How can mist exist in this strong wind? It didn't make sense. It seemed to hang suspended in the air, unchanged by the violent wind. All those days she'd spent here last year with Danny, Rob, and her grandfather, she'd never seen this before.

She turned on her flashlight and shone it up ahead of her. It still looked like mist, but in the strong beam of her light she could see that is actually *was* moving, just not as one big entity carried on the wind. It seemed to be pulsating, or perhaps swirling … and not as a whole, but in small patches, in some synchronized pattern. Everywhere she shone her light the mist was doing the same strange dance. When she got close, the mist disappeared or parted, only to regroup ahead, always seemingly a few feet away.

Though it was mesmerizing, Christy forced herself to put it out of her mind for the time being to pick the direction she would continue in. Even though the sound was bearable, she knew that even if she yelled, the chances of Cory hearing her over the wind were slim, so she just flashed her light off into the dark in all directions as she walked. Making a wide circle with the spot she and Cory had used for protection from the wind as the center point, she did a full lap around, waving her flashlight all the while. Each time she came to the starting point, she headed further away from the center and walked in a widening circle. Each successive circle was more difficult, as the terrain she had to walk over was increasingly dotted with obstacles— mostly small boulders and stunted, thick-stalked plants. After walking that way for many rotations, she was forced to admit that she really didn't know where the center point was anymore. Frustration set in, so she just walked straight out from her best guess of where the starting point had been, waving the flashlight over her head.

Suddenly she saw an answering flash of light in the distance. It blinked off and on in a regular pattern. If it was Cory, then he was signaling to her. She walked through the dark, keeping her focus on the distant light. When it stopped, she shone her light off and on into the sky and the answering light returned for her to follow. After fifteen minutes following the light, it was finally getting close. The strange mist and the darkness made it difficult to see any identifying landmarks. Christy slowed down her pace and noticed that the light was getting closer even when she was standing still.

"Is that you, Cory?" Christy yelled, hoping the light holder was close enough to hear above the wind.

"Walker?" came the reply.

"Here!" she yelled.

Cory emerged from the dark, looking as defiant as ever when Christy shone her light in his face. He shielded his eyes from the beam.

"I would have been back," he said. "You didn't have to come looking for me."

"You're correct there— I shouldn't have come looking," she replied. "Then when you didn't come back, I could have gone on by myself and not been responsible for you."

"I'm responsible for myself, Walker. I don't need you to babysit me," Cory said.

"You know, you keep telling me you don't need me, but we both know that's not true. So, what's the saying ... 'Let's agree to disagree,'" Christy said. "I just saw another spot to rest for the night that's protected a bit. We better wait until daylight so I can figure out where we are and get us back on the path to Clacker's hut."

She led Cory to the spot and the two of them settled down and tried to get as much sleep as they could. Christy tossed and turned, having slept a good part of the afternoon away. Finally, she fell asleep, and when she woke up in the morning, the sky was brightening.

As soon as it was light enough, Christy shook Cory who, to his credit, didn't protest. They got up, hefted their packs, and were on their way. Christy took the lead; she walked so the wind was at her back, then started the same routine she'd done the night before of walking in increasing circles— this time in hopes of seeing some familiar landmark. She searched for over an hour with Cory walking sometimes behind her and sometimes by her side. Taking a break, she stopped and set down her pack.

Cory did the same. "What's the problem? Where are we?"

Christy stared at Cory through squinted eyes. "You know, you are the one who got us into this situation. I haven't seen anything that looks familiar yet."

"Me? I told you last night if you'd stayed put, I'd have been back."

"If you'd stayed put," Christy mocked. "We both know you're full of it. You had no chance of finding your way back." Then after a pause she said, "If you could have, you would have. You were gone a long time. So I had to come looking for you. And if you would have been able to last night, then get us back now to where we started from, know-it-all. Go ahead, because otherwise, we're lost."

Cory stared at her for a second then averted his eyes. "Well, you've got me all confused now with your walking in circles."

Christy exhaled loudly and threw up her hands. "Just what I figured, you haven't a clue where we are."

Cory snickered, and Christy reacted immediately. "You think it's funny? I don't know where we are."

CHAPTER 10

They walked for hours in the ever-widening circles without Christy ever seeing anything familiar. With each passing moment and new unfamiliar scene that presented itself, Christy felt more and more as if she'd ruined their chances. Finally, she put up her hands and called a halt to their now aimless wandering.

"I have no idea how to get us back." She sat down on the spongy ground and burst into tears. Cory didn't say anything— he just stood over her, not even taking the opportunity to sit.

After a few minutes, Christy wiped her eyes and stood up. "We have to keep walking," she said, and perhaps because he had no other ideas, Cory didn't protest. They walked for quite a while in silence before they entered a noise area and were forced to put ear protection on. When they climbed a small rise in the landscape and she still didn't see anything she recognized, Christy promptly sat down and started to cry again. She had been banking on seeing something from the higher vantage point, and the disappointment she felt was crushing. Cory sat down beside her and waited for her to calm down.

After about ten minutes of resting, Christy was about to resume their walking— though she had no idea which way to go— when Cory tapped her on the shoulder. He was pantomiming something by tapping the spongy moss beneath them, but Christy shrugged her shoulders, not understanding. Cory then flattened himself on the moss, with his ear pressed into it. He motioned for Christy to do the same. Curious as to what he might be getting at, she put her own head to the ground.

At first she didn't understand, but then she noticed something. Through her right shoulder pressed to the ground, and even through her ear protection, she felt an odd vibration. She focused on it and it began to take on a rhythm, a routine pattern. It came and went like a pulse. She sat up and placed her hands down on the spongy moss. Now that she was looking for it, she felt it through her hands also.

Cory stared at her and Christy shrugged her shoulders. She had no idea what it was, but that was the second different thing she'd experienced since she got back to the Empty World—the strange, wind resistant mist being the first. When she couldn't offer Cory any explanation of what it was, he quickly seemed to lose interest.

After a few more minutes of resting, Christy tapped Cory on the shoulder to keep going, though at that point, she wasn't confident they'd find their way back to the path to Clacker's place. She decided to change her tactics by picking the direction with the wind at their backs and heading out. In the distance she saw a few rises and falls to the land and figured that at the crest of any of those small hills there may be a view of something she'd recognize. It was all she had for a plan, so she ignored her fear and kept on walking, only occasionally glancing back to make sure Cory was following.

At the crest of the third small hill, Christy sensed something was familiar but realized quickly it was only that she was getting good at identifying the subtle changes in the landscape that signaled either a return to a dangerous noise area or the ending of one. For whatever reason, where the sound was dangerous, the plants growing in those areas had much smaller leaves.

All the trees and shrubs across the world had thick leathery foliage, probably due to the strong unending wind, but in places where the sound was brutal, the plants had adapted smaller, thicker foliage, and some even had none. Christy didn't understand why the noise would have affected the plants even more so than the wind, but she definitely noticed its effects.

This area they were starting to enter on the descent of the small slope had that subtle change to the plants that signaled an end to a noise area.

Christy was walking with little hope of anything at this point— she realized they were probably miles away from anything familiar, and it was time to have a serious talk with Cory about their next move.

Christy stopped to wait for Cory, who was lagging a dozen or so yards behind, and removed her ear protection. When Cory caught up, he did the same.

"What are we going to do? Just keep walking?" Cory asked, hands planted on his hips.

"You got a better idea, Daniel Boone?"

"Yeah, how about ... don't get lost."

Christy immediately changed her mind about the talk, turned, and left Cory behind again.

Danny followed last in line. Clacker was in the lead with Brad right behind him. Danny was struggling to keep up to the two; with their longer legs, they ate up more ground with each stride.

Danny watched Brad stumble a few times up ahead. He suspected that Brad hadn't slept too well. He seemed to be a creature of habit, and his sleeping habits at home included having his brother in the other bed in his room. Clacker glanced back numerous times during their trek, and Danny saw the Cleaner's obvious concern for his human charges—Brad stumbling and Danny himself falling far back at times and then running to keep up. Finally, Clacker waved a halt and the two boys sat down.

Danny was grateful for the rest and took the opportunity to really look at his surroundings for the first time since they had escaped from the ancients. The plants here were much taller than other places in this strange world; they almost looked like real trees, although without much in the way of leaves. Leathery strips of multicolored vegetation snaked up from the ground along the leeward side of the sturdier trunks, just as Danny remembered, but these plants towered over them.

The sound was almost non-existent in that area, so Brad and Clacker had removed their sound protectors. Danny noticed Brad out of the corner of his eye. He was prone on the ground, with the right side of his head pressed down deep into the moss.

Danny risked Brad's negative reaction by tapping him on the leg, and Brad sat up with only a slight flinch. Danny signed, "What?"

By way of response, Brad signed and spoke, "It's stronger here."

Danny was sure he'd read Brad's lips right and had understood his signs, but he was puzzled by the comment. "What's stronger?"

"I can hear it now," Brad said aloud. Then he put his head down again into the moss. Danny stared puzzled for a moment, and then emulated Brad for lack of other ideas.

The second he pressed his own head down into the moss, he knew. Even without hearing, he could feel the vibration and could imagine that Brad might hear something coming from it. He sat up and got Clacker's attention.

"Do you know what that is?" Danny signed. He tapped the moss and briefly pressed his head down again before sitting up and looking to Clacker for his answer.

Clacker crudely signed and said, "The power under the land."

Danny tapped Brad again, who flinched away from the touch and didn't raise his head, so Danny asked out loud, "Brad, what did Clacker say?"

"I hear metal," he said, as Danny read his lips.

"Is that what Clacker said?" Danny asked. Brad slowly shook his head. "Do you hear metal?" Brad nodded.

Clacker pointed off into the wind. "The power is close to us," he signed. "My ancestors have told me. We have felt the power for generations. I have never been this close."

Danny was baffled. Was the vibration in the ground from metal? Or from some enigmatic power that Clacker's ancestors were familiar with? And if so, what was that power from?

"Any of this useful, Walker?" Cory called from behind her. With the wind at their backs, his voice carried loud and clear and just as annoying as always.

`Christy stopped and waited for him to catch up. "We just have to keep the wind at our backs and keep going in the same direction I went with my grandfather. Eventually we'll get somewhere I recognize."

"You know, if I wasn't so tired, I'm sure I'd find some flaw in that." Cory let his pack drop onto the moss before sliding down to rest. Christy didn't object; in fact, she was also getting tired and welcomed it.

Christy sat down near Cory and put her head down. This was the perfect time for a rest. They'd been up since early dawn and had walked miles—unproductive miles at that, since Christy still hadn't seen anything that looked familiar. Despite her assurances to Cory, she was beginning to doubt herself and her confident statements about eventually finding familiar landmarks.

In fact, this area and most of what they'd traveled through during the whole day so far looked much different than what she'd been used to in the Empty World. Yes, the moss was still covering the ground and for the most part it was the same dull tan color she was used to, but the rest of the vegetation appeared to diverge from the norm. Their forms were larger. They still twisted around each other for better fortitude against the wind, and any foliage was thick and rubbery and on the leeward side of the trunks, but the size of them was beginning to be impressive.

They had walked through groups of what Christy would almost call trees, and not just in protected areas behind large rock outcroppings. For whole stretches of rolling terrain, Christy and Cory had walked through actual forested land. The larger and more numerous the tall plants became, the more firm the moss. It didn't roll and give and sink under their feet. Christy's grandfather had hated that moss for its "determined sucking ability" as he'd called it. More than once last year, they'd all cried out in frustration as the moss fought them every step of the way.

This time, Cory was enough of a challenge to deal with, and Christy was glad that the moss was not as bad of a problem.

Despite that one positive note in their favor, and the impressive scenery, Christy was getting down on herself. If she didn't find something familiar soon, she was in danger of throwing in the towel and pronouncing them hopelessly lost.

Cory was reclined next to her, using the moss as a pillow when suddenly he sat upright. "That weird vibration is getting annoying."

Christy put her head down just as Cory had done. "Oh, I don't know, I kind of think it's relaxing." She let the vibration soothe away her fatigue.

"What's that?" Cory asked.

Christy, tired and relaxing in the deep moss and the vibration, ignored him.

"Walker, what's that?" He shook her into full attention.

Christy sat up ready to yell at him for disturbing her but then she saw he was pointing at something.

There was an outcropping way off in the distance. She guessed that it was bigger than any outcropping she'd seen yet on this world. She wouldn't call it a mountain, but in comparison to the mostly rolling, moss covered land, it was huge and towered over the surrounding landscape.

CHAPTER 11

The door to Trevor's room opened.

"He's in here, Ginny," Trevor's mom said.

"Thanks, Mrs. Hanson."

Trevor looked up without any real interest as his mom closed the door behind Ginny Wentworth, one of his two best friends. He acknowledged she was in the room with a slight nod.

Ginny sat down on the bed next to him and smiled. She tried to give him a hug— something she'd been doing every time she'd seen him since the previous summer. Trevor usually endured them, but today he pulled away. She didn't press the issue, but instead sat there silently. A minute later, the silence became awkward enough that Trevor finally looked at her.

"What? Did my mom ask you to come here to cheer me up?"

"No, I came because I just heard about everything. Your mom called last night to tell us about everyone going through the pond again."

"Not everyone," Trevor shot back quickly.

"So, you told your parents about our plans," Ginny stated.

"Yeah, had to. Mrs. Peters was trying to say that Christy must have recruited the twins to go with her. And you and I know that isn't true. I obviously had to say that Christy and I planned to go together. But I kept you out of it. I didn't tell them that you were planning along with us— that you were going to be the one staying here after Christy and I left so you could tell everyone we'd gone back to rescue her grandfather. I've been grounded since. But at least Mrs. Peters found notes that Cory wrote about supplies and plans that he and Brad were making on their own, so she's not blaming Christy anymore."

"Well, thanks for trying to leave me out of it but I told my parents I was planning to help you. I'm grounded too."

Trevor finally looked her in the eye. "Why? You should have kept yourself out of it."

"I couldn't let you take all the blame. I've been let out of my solitary confinement just long enough to apologize to Christy's mom and come see you. My mom says the only way I get to do anything this summer is if I can help get them back. I don't see that happening. We know where a working portal is, we just have to wait."

Trevor stared down at his hands. "I just can't believe they went without me. That just doesn't make any sense at all. Christy would never have gone with the twins for any reason." He looked at Ginny, expecting her to agree with him, but she kept quiet. "Last year when she came back we talked a lot about why she went without me. It made sense then, even though I didn't like it. Someone had to be here to explain everything. But not this time. You know, while we planned this, we didn't even consider needing someone here to convince people the portal exists and nobody'd drowned. No, there's no way at all that going with the twins or Danny was part of a plan by Christy. Something really bad must have happened, and she got in the middle of it."

"You might be right, but what can we do about it?" Ginny asked.

Trevor let out an exasperated sigh. "I don't know. They won't tell me anything, but I know something is up. I haven't seen Christy's dad since Christy disappeared; his car hasn't left the driveway and I'm pretty sure Detective Lockhart's car is parked there too. But I've only been by there twice since I've been grounded."

"If that is Detective Lockhart's car, don't you think he'd at least stop and say hi to you? You came to him first with everything last year and he rallied all of us together. I traveled to France with him."

Trevor was silent for a moment, nodding his head. "Yeah, I know. Like I said, something is going on that they're not telling us. I wish I knew what it was."

"Do you notice it, Walker?"

"Yeah, through my feet. And that hum *is* getting annoying," Christy acknowledged. The outcropping loomed large overhead, casting a deep shadow on their path. Christy and Cory were slowly approaching it, wary of the now strong vibration and the hum, which despite the relentless wind, was loud enough that they were constantly conscious of it.

Christy was in the lead, and as they approached the flat cliff-like face to the outcropping, she looked around for a tunnel opening. Dark shadows stretched out from a gap in the face, and Christy saw it was the opening she had hoped for.

"I don't think this is a good idea, Walker," Cory said to her back as he followed behind her. For a second, she ignored him, but then she turned.

"Why not? I would think this is exactly what you planned to come here for." Cory stood looking at the looming overhang they were now standing under.

"Have you ever seen or heard anything else like this here?"

"No," Christy admitted. "Never an entrance to a tunnel making a noise like a factory of some kind. But we're lost. What have we got to lose?"

"You're not just going to walk inside, are you?"

"No," she said, and Cory let out a sigh of relief. The rhythmic gear sounds surrounded them, seeming to vibrate and radiate right out of the stone itself. Christy looked into the opening and then back at Cory. "You're coming with me," she said. And with that she turned her back and started for the opening, pulling her flashlight out of her pack.

She didn't wait for a reply as she entered the tunnel. Within mere seconds she saw light up ahead and put her flashlight away. Cory caught up with her as she came to a stop.

"Do you think we should put our ear protection on? That hum is getting louder," Cory said.

"No, this is nothing like the deadly sound we pass in and out of outside," Christy answered. "But it is weird, and now I think I can hear some sort of metal clanking. Do you hear that?"

"Yeah, bang, bang then something grinding maybe, and then it repeats," Cory said. "How come your grandfather never told you about this?"

"He couldn't have known about this or I'm sure he would have said something. We have to find out what is making those sounds and the vibration."

"Whoa, Walker, I think we need to turn around now and get out of here. I don't need to see what's up ahead. There's enough outside that I've already seen to impress anyone at home."

"We're going forward, not back," Christy said.

"Remember, Walker, you're not in charge."

"You want to get home, don't you?"

"And how are you going to get us there? We're lost, and you have no idea how to get us to the working portal, so again, you're not in charge here. I'm turning around."

"Then wait for me here at the entrance, or leave and find your own way to the portal. I don't care either way."

Christy turned and continued down the tunnel, getting closer to where the factory sounds and the vibrations were coming from.

The path was quickly looking like the tunnels in all the other outcroppings she'd been in. The light was diffused, seemingly coming from nowhere, and the floor was solid stone. The walls seemed to conduct the sound well. As she rounded each turn she expected to see what was making the noise, but it seemed to be much farther in than she had expected.

The hum was starting to separate into a few distinct sounds. A metallic banging noise kept a uniform rhythm, and then there was a background noise that Christy thought sounded like a clothes dryer spinning. The walls vibrated when she touched them; it was just like what they'd felt through the moss for the last few miles, only it was much more pronounced, even shaking the floor under her feet.

Christy walked for a while, keeping her eyes on the way ahead until she arrived at a doorway in the tunnel that blocked her from going further. It was the first door Christy had seen in this world other than the massive door to the return portal. She approached it and it hummed all on its own, startling her to stop short. As she watched it, it began to slide into the wall, but stopped with a grinding sound once it was halfway open.

Beyond the partially opened door, Christy could see what looked like a short platform ending with a set of metal bars or a waist high railing. It was what she could barely glimpse just past the railing that really caught her attention. All of the sounds and the vibration were definitely emanating from there. Christy moved a step closer and peeked through the door; then she squeezed through the partial opening onto a landing. She was in awe of what was in front of her.

She stood on a platform high above a massive room. The term "room" didn't even do what she was looking at justice—it was expansive. She looked up. The ceiling was a good twenty feet above her even though the platform she was on was already four or five stories above the floor. The room stretched off so far that she couldn't see the other end. As impressive as its size, its contents were even more intriguing.

The grinding sounds and background hum came from the wheels, pistons and whirling gears, which filled the room and stretched up the walls into the distance. Blue ceramic paved pathways wound their way through the metropolis of functioning machines. One main pathway stretched off and disappeared along with the end of the room. Lights blinked and pulsated from the thousands of machines but there was little extra light illuminating the room. It looked like an enclosed city, partially sleeping.

"Holy cow. What is this?" Cory asked as he came up behind her.

Christy grinned when she felt Cory there, but then the enormity of what they were looking at hit her. "I don't know," she whispered. To be heard over the sounds of the room, she added more loudly, "My grandfather thought the sound was from the wind from the glaciers coming down through a mountain with a hole weathered through it. But I bet this has a lot more to do with it."

With his camera in hand, Cory stepped beside Christy and took snapshot after snapshot. Despite her previous threat, she let him take as many pictures as he wanted.

"So maybe there's still a lot more people here than you thought," Cory said.

"Maybe, but I don't see anyone, do you?" she asked in a whisper, suddenly nervous. "Maybe it just runs without anyone keeping it going." Christy leaned over the railing and looked down, then into the distance to see if she could see anything through the relative darkness. "I don't see a way down there. This can't be the main entrance."

Cory turned and looked up above the door they'd squeezed through. "Look!" he said, pointing.

Christy turned and followed his gaze up. Metal rungs in the stone trailed up the wall. Halfway to the ceiling they ended at what appeared to be an opening. As Christy gazed around the room, she saw that there were other openings spaced at set intervals which continued for as far as she could see into the distance.

Cory was also eyeing the other openings. "Have you ever been to the Hoover Dam?" he asked.

Christy frowned. "No. Why?"

"I'll bet this is a maintenance entrance," Cory said. "We took a vacation two years ago to the Hoover Dam, and it had all these maintenance entrances. You can't get there as a tourist, but the workers can. And in Boston the South Station tunnel has all these openings along it that workers use for maintenance too."

Christy nodded. She had seen the openings at South Station and these did look similar.

Christy turned again towards the rungs overhead and tried to jump to reach the closest one, but it was just out of her reach. "Give me a boost up," she said.

"No," Cory said, shaking his head, arms crossed over his chest. "Not on your life, Walker. Let's go."

"Why? What's the harm?" Christy pleaded. "If this room is the cause of the sound and wind, I want to find a way to shut it off."

"What are you, out of your mind? If you're right, this has probably been running for thousands of years. Do you think you're going to find out how to shut all this off? It looks like this room is larger than any football stadium I've ever seen on TV. That's a whole lot of machines out there."

"Come on, help me up to that rung. You can wait here if you want."

Cory shook his head. "You know what, Walker? I used to think you were the smartest kid in our grade, but you are either crazy or have a lot less brains than I thought, if you think it's a good idea to go exploring in here. We need to get out of here now, not fool around with heavy machinery. Let's just find our way to the working portal." Cory put his hands on his hips and stared straight at Christy. "And even though I probably do need you to get back home alive, I'll just have to take my chances out there if you're gonna stay poking around in here." Cory turned and started to squeeze out through the doorway.

Christy looked up at the rung that was just out of reach and stomped her foot. Before Cory had squeezed through the door she gave him a little push and squeezed out after him.

They walked back along the tunnel in mostly silence.

"Ginny's way smarter than me," Christy said, finally.

Cory grimaced, or maybe he smiled— Christy couldn't tell the difference. "Yeah, I know. But it got you out of there, didn't it?"

CHAPTER 12

Ever since their decision to postpone heading to the portal in order to go towards "the power of the land," Clacker had been shaking. His protective clothes as well as the short knives and small club strapped to his belt all looked as if they were dancing. They were shaking so rapidly that when Danny tried staring at any of them, his eyes were unable to focus. Was Clacker nervous? Excited?

Clacker led at a faster pace than they were used to. The moss underfoot seemed more rigid and the walking was less tiring because of it. They came to the top of a slope, and off about a mile in the distance across several more gentle rises and falls of the land, a large outcropping peaked up over the landscape. Brad stopped abruptly when he saw it and took off his ear protectors. Danny stopped too, afraid he'd bump into Brad.

When he saw the two boys stopped, Clacker walked back to meet them. When he reached the boys, he began crudely signing and moving his mouth. Danny had trouble with the signs, so he asked Brad what Clacker had said, but he found that Brad was not paying any attention— he was staring intently at the ground. Clacker saw and gently pinched Brad, his mouth moving even faster. For some reason, Clacker's touch didn't affect Brad as much as when Danny tried to get his attention, but Brad continued to ignore whatever it was that Clacker had said. Finally, Clacker slapped his pinchers together and appeared to be yelling.

Brad looked up. "Clacker warns us to either keep going towards the portal or quickly go towards the 'power of the land,'" Brad said. "The longer we stand here, the greater the chance that the ancients searching for us will find us."

"I agree with Clacker, Brad. Why did you stop?" Danny asked. But Brad was again staring at the ground and Danny was unsure if he'd answer.

Finally, Brad glanced up and then down at the ground again. "I have to go there," he said, and turned to point at the large outcropping.

Danny was confused. "That's where we're going anyway, Brad. Why? Did you see something?"

Brad didn't answer, just dropped his eyes to the ground again and stood there. Clacker's mouth moved, and he touched Brad again.

"Cory is there," Brad said, and started walking in the direction he'd pointed.

Danny grabbed Brad to stop him. "Cory? How do you know that?"

Brad shook off Danny's grip. "I can see his footprints."

Danny looked down at the moss—he didn't see any footprints.

"Where?" he asked. But Brad was already too far ahead to hear him. Clacker threw up his pinchers in a remarkably human gesture of frustration and took off after Brad. Danny shook his head and raced to keep up.

A quarter of a mile after breaking out of the shadow of the overhang and into the bright sun, Christy and Cory were bickering again, and she was on the verge of tears.

"Just please shut up. Our situation wouldn't suck so much if we could just walk in silence."

She was several paces in front of Cory and grateful when he didn't respond.

As they walked away from the entirely alien place they'd encountered— Cory trailing behind— Christy was berating herself for not sticking to her guns, not telling Cory to go ahead without her if he didn't want to try to explore what they'd stumbled upon. She focused her eyes on the ground in front of her, and when she finally looked up, the trail was clear for the length of a football field or more before it rose up slightly, hiding any further view beyond.

Over that rise, a figure came into view. Christy froze for a moment, unsure of what to do. Cory came up behind her and she felt him stop, bumping into her slightly. She was about to tell Cory that they should hide off the trail, or run, when the figure came into clear view in definitely human form and broke towards them in a run.

"Brad?" she finally said, a smile spreading across her face. Right behind Brad, two more figures came over the rise. "Danny? Clacker?" Christy started to run towards the group. Cory hesitated only a second then followed behind her.

It took only a few seconds for the two groups running towards each other to meet along the path. Danny practically tackled Christy who hung onto him fiercely for a second. Cory had stopped short, eyeing the strange creature that was Clacker even though he'd been told about him, and even seen a sketch. Brad went right up to Cory and put his arms around him.

Seeing this, Christy smiled. "I've never seen Brad hug anyone before," she said.

Cory tried to step back but Brad had him tight, so he pushed to free himself.

"He's never hugged anyone, not even my mom," he said.

Brad stood looking down at the ground between him and Cory. "I came first to wait for you. Danny made me leave," he said.

Danny, who was straining to follow Brad's lips, said, "We were captured by Angry Ancient. Clacker was captured too and he helped up escape."

They took an impromptu rest, settling down in a circle. Christy listened and watched as Danny told her and Cory about following Brad and then being captured, meeting Clacker and their subsequent escape. When Danny described their sightless escape from the Ancients, he pantomimed his confused flight led by Clacker's touch, and they all laughed.

It struck her that even though they all were in a strange world, and some of them had even been taken prisoner by aliens, that they could recount their adventures and laugh while doing it.

"Have you seen my grandfather?" Christy interrupted and slipped almost seamlessly into signing again as she spoke.

Danny shook his head. Christy frowned, tears welling up again.

"What about Clacker? Has he seen my grandfather?"

Danny tapped Brad and said. "Ask Clacker if he's seen Jack?"

Brad started to vocalize strange sounds, then stopped, out of breath.

Christy couldn't believe it. Could he actually be talking with Clacker?

To her surprise, Clacker began his crude signing and spoke with his clicking language, staring at Christy, clearly trying to tell her his part of the story. Christy shook her head frustrated and unsure what Clacker was signing.

"Brad, can you tell Christy what Clacker just said?" Danny prompted.

Brad hesitated but then said, "Clacker came looking for anyone who might be coming back to look for Jack. He waited at Jack's cave then found us near the portal where we were all captured."

"Brad, that's amazing," Christy said. "How did you learn that so quickly?"

Brad frowned. "I need to get better." Christy laughed. Cory shook his head. "You should see some of the crazy things he's good at," he said.

Christy shook her head. "I wouldn't call this crazy. It's incredible. Has he really learned Clacker's language that fast?"

Danny nodded and smiled.

They all stood up to continue on when Cory stepped over to his brother and gave him a shove so hard that Brad stumbled back a step.

"You're such a jerk," Cory yelled at him. "It's your fault they're here. If you'd waited for me, we'd have come here by ourselves. How stupid can you get?"

Christy stepped between the brothers. "Leave him alone," she said. She tried to quickly change the subject and distract Brad at the same time. "Clacker, can you help us get to the working portal and to the village of the ancients near there?" She had to sign to Brad to prompt him to relay her question.

Clacker nodded his head while speaking to Brad, and then nudged Brad with his pincher. When he did, Brad spoke up.

"Clacker says he can get us to the swamp and as long as one of us knows how to get to the village or the working portal from there, we'll be fine."

Christy felt the urgency of an opportunity slipping past her, so she told the group what she and Cory had discovered. Danny explained that he'd been heading for the same outcropping. The question now became whether they would return to explore it or continue on to the portal to home.

Cory made it clear that his vote was for heading to the working portal immediately. When nobody said anything opposing him right away, they all picked up their packs and were about to start when Christy spoke up.

"Danny and I both probably remember how to get to the glider once on the other side of the swamp. You'll—"

She paused, choosing her words carefully. "The village has to be close by. It shouldn't be hard to find."

Danny stared at Christy for a second then signed something rapidly. It was what had earned him the nickname of Flying Fingers from Cory. Christy frowned at him— nobody had followed the signing, not even Brad, so she waved for him to halt and asked him to start again, slower.

Danny slowed it down and spoke aloud, his voice quivering. "You did this to Trevor, now you're trying to do it to me, aren't you?"

Christy averted Danny's eyes and kept silent.

"What is he talking about, Walker?" Cory asked.

Neither Christy nor Danny responded, so Cory grabbed Danny by the arm and turned him around so they were facing. "What are you talking about, Shrimp?"

"Christy isn't coming with us," Danny replied. "Right, Christy?" He turned momentarily back to look at Christy, then looked at Cory again and said, "She forced Trevor to stay back when she came here the first time by saying he had to stay and tell everyone where she'd gone. Now she's saying I can find the glider, not that 'we' can find the glider. She knows the way just as well as I do." Turning again to face Christy, he added, "What are you going to do? You can't seriously think you're going back alone to try to get into whatever you saw back there, do you?"

Cory, Brad, and Clacker were staring at Christy. She squirmed uncomfortably under the weight of their eyes. Cory's eyes narrowed as if her intention had finally dawned on him.

"That's exactly what she's doing," he said. "You're going back there, alone, aren't you?"

Christy looked up finally and exhaled. She realized she had been holding her breath. "I have to explore that massive room ... I have to go back."

Danny signed a translation of Christy's words for Clacker, since she hadn't bothered to. The alien nodded and replied, and Danny prompted Brad to translate for the rest of the group.

"Clacker says he's going forward," Brad said. "That since we are so close, we all should see what's in there. He wants to see the legend that he's heard about his whole life. His ancestors called it the power of the land."

"Who cares what's in there?" Cory asked. "We should just walk away. If Walker wants to go back, let her. I don't want to follow her."

Christy argued. "I guess if Clacker wants to see it too, we should all go. But I definitely have to go back. What if that place controls the sound and maybe even the wind? Clacker just called it 'the power of the land.' Sounds to me like it controls everything. If I can turn that off, this place wouldn't be so deadly."

"Even if you find a way down to the main level, what makes you think you can find out how to turn everything off, assuming it is run from there?" Cory argued.

"I'm sure I can find some kind of a ladder, or maybe Clacker can give me a boost up or something. And we'll just have to hope we find what we're looking for, even if we don't know what that is just yet."

Cory tried to spit on the ground, but the wind broke it into a million drops before it hit the moss. He was about to counter Christy's comments when Clacker started clicking again.

They all looked at Brad when Clacker finished. Without any prompting Brad said, "Clacker wants us to make up our minds quickly. The ancients we escaped from are probably after us."

Then Brad tugged on Cory's sleeve. "Cory, can we go home now? I don't like it here."

Brad's question swayed them all. Cory was going to get his way. He wasn't going back with Christy. But Danny wouldn't hear anything about her going alone.

"I'm going with you," Danny said adamantly.

"Danny, you can't. Cory and Brad need someone to lead them to the working portal. Clacker has said he can only get us to the swamp. One of us has to know the way beyond that."

Clacker clicked a series of responses and his body stopped its strange vibrations.

Brad interpreted Clackers response. "He says although he's disappointed, he will accept his role and lead us while Christy and Danny go forward. We will wait at the swamp till Christy and Danny meet up with us."

CHAPTER 13

While they were standing on the platform overlooking the massive room, which stretched off into the distance humming and clanging and glowing with a thousand different points of light, Christy hugged Danny impulsively.

"I'm glad you're here," she said. As soon as Clacker led the twins off to find the swamp, Christy had eagerly pulled Danny by the hand to where they now stood.

"We need to find something to help us both get up there," Danny said, pointing at the doorway opening above the platform.

"You can boost me up. I'm not too heavy," Christy signed.

"Then I'd be stuck here," Danny said. "We either find a way for both of us to go, or we leave and catch up to the others."

Christy hesitated, then nodded. "Well," she began, "there's nothing for us to stand on here, so let's look outside for something."

Danny agreed, and they went back out through the jammed doorway toward daylight. Once outside, they searched along the path they'd come down, but remembering that useful items were scarce on it, eventually decided to investigate a small side path through a thick stand of plants. After about a mile, they emerged into a wide-open area where the moss was beaten down and the footing was almost as solid as a wood floor. The network of bamboo-like pipes that dominated the clearing was something they were familiar with. It was a delivery system like the one Christy's grandfather had used to contact Clacker, except this one only stretched off for a hundred yards or so before it ended in disrepair. Pieces of piping were missing from the structure, other lengths of piping were broken, and the whole thing had clearly been abandoned. Some of the bamboo had a dark growth on it, which obscured the shininess of the wood beneath it. As they approached the closest section of the structure, small animals darted out of some of the holes.

With a quick oily spray, the furry animals rolled up and were blown off into the growth beyond. Christy and Danny both recognized the marsupials as the same creatures that Christy's grandfather had shown them were used to deliver messages through the bamboo. They were the same as the creature that Danny had witnessed the ancients torture.

"Like a cluster of billiard balls scattering," Danny said after they watched the critters' frightened retreats. Christy laughed at his observation. The whole thing struck her as a comical display of evolution taking advantage of a long-standing pattern of weather.

"This is perfect," Danny said as he hurried ahead. He searched his way through the bamboo and picked up short pieces, putting them aside. After some fifteen minutes passed, Danny had gathered what he needed and took a roll of twine out of his pack.

"Let me help." Christy offered.

"I'm good. Just when I start lashing the rungs, if you could hold them steady, that'd be great."

While Danny worked, he and Christy talked about their last time in the Empty World.

"I wonder what happened to the pistol my grandfather gave to Rob as we got on the glider," Christy said. "All the time we were guarded by the ancients in front of the door, we never asked him where it was. Not that I think any of us would have been able to use it."

"I might have been able to use it on Angry Ancient," Danny said.

Christy smiled. "But what happened to it?"

"I asked him that once. He was over early for a lesson and you guys hadn't shown up yet. He thought maybe he dropped it when your grandfather pushed us in the glider and Rob had to cut the side ropes. He didn't remember having it after that."

The conversation lulled as they lost themselves in thought, and Christy admired the ladder that Danny had assembled. It was made up of two long sections of bamboo set parallel to each other with notches cut up the lengths for the shorter cross pieces.

"Wow, looks great," Christy said as Danny raised the ladder to its full height. "Thanks. Can you step on the bottom rung? If that holds, then all of them should."

Christy climbed onto the bottom step while Danny held the ladder, bracing himself. Bouncing on it slightly, she tested it to make sure it wouldn't snap on them. It creaked slightly but seemed reassuringly solid under her feet. She stepped off of it and clapped her hands, feeling as if they had found the key to a treasure chest and were just moments away from discovering what it held.

Satisfied that the ladder would hold them both, they set about dragging it back along the way they'd come. Despite their early enthusiasm, it still wasn't easy. The spongy moss resisted their efforts, and they had to repeatedly stop to rest. By the time they finally got the ladder in place on the platform, they were both exhausted but more eager to explore than ever.

Christy was about to start up the ladder to the opening above when Danny grabbed her arm.

"What is it, Danny?" she asked.

"We don't know what we'll find up there. Let's agree to not split up, ok?"

Christy nodded. "Agreed," she said, and stepped up onto their ladder. After a few more steps, she grabbed hold of the lowest metal rung above her head and used the rungs to climb the rest of the way to the opening. She stepped through it and found herself in a tunnel illuminated by a soft glow. She turned to wave down to Danny and he climbed up after her.

Standing side by side in the tunnel, they paused while their eyes adjusted to the low light. The passageway itself seemed faintly luminous, and the soft light emanating from it allowed them to keep their flashlights off as long as they walked slowly. Keeping close together, they walked past several of the openings that overlooked the floor below. It seemed Cory was right about them all being connected as they would be in a maintenance tunnel, Christy thought. After they'd been walking past the openings for a while, they came upon an open archway on the opposite wall; no light of any kind emanated from beyond it— it was a gaping black hole. Christy turned on her flashlight and shone it through, revealing a descending staircase beyond that disappeared around a corner.

Meeting eyes, the two of them nodded to each other and quietly headed down the stairs. Despite being cut into the stone of the hillside, the passageway was neither cold nor damp. Like every other passageway they'd seen in the Empty World, this one defied all logic. Their flashlights illuminated their way, but just barely— the beams traveled only far enough to light two stairs beyond their next step. Christy couldn't figure out how the light just stopped. It was as if it were trying to reach its potential but gave up after three or four feet. Christy turned her light toward Danny to confirm its odd behavior. Sure enough, he cast no shadow on the wall. She tried making shadow puppets. That test too failed. Danny nodded. It seemed he had noticed the same thing. Since she couldn't see far ahead, Christy tried to listen closely with each step, but stopped abruptly as something else dawned on her.

Their footsteps—they weren't making any noise! Danny touched her sleeve and looked at her questioningly, but Christy just shrugged and shook her head. On an impulse, she yelled out. The noise was absorbed immediately, without even the hint of an echo. Christy grinned and beckoned Danny to keep walking, waving off his confusion. The eerie lack of an echo was lost on him and Christy didn't want to stop to explain. They crept slowly, afraid that by hurrying they'd get ahead of their flashlight beams, but Christy was more impatient than ever to find out where the stairs would lead.

Finally, after what felt like a hundred steps or more, the staircase ended, flattening out into a passageway. Almost immediately they noticed the light again—it was emanating from maddeningly impossible to pinpoint sources and it allowed them to keep their flashlights off as they followed the narrow passageway.

Christy figured they were walking parallel to the enormous room with the strange machines in it. She hoped that eventually they'd come to a doorway opening into it, but instead the passage seemed to bend off to the left, away from their destination. Though frustrated, Christy noticed the tunnel seemed to widen up ahead and grow darker. Just as she was about to switch her flashlight on, she froze as three circular lighting columns on the wall cast the area in a clear, white light. They had entered into a room, about the size of Christy's living room back home, with the walls and ceiling a flat cream color.

The interior of the room looked like some sort of museum, as along one wall were the first artifacts they'd seen anywhere in the Empty World. Hanging from bright silver hooks and spaced about a foot apart were metallic, aqua blue garments that looked like overcoats and reflected the light, shimmering almost as if they were moving. Christy went over to one of them and touched the fabric. It felt as soft as the silk of her mom's handkerchiefs, but as thick as heavy canvas. Christy lifted it up off the hook.

"What on earth! Danny, feel this," she exclaimed. "It feels lighter than a tee-shirt, but look how thick it is! And it's the size of a trench coat. How is that possible?"

Danny took the coat from her and hefted it up and down. He then folded it neatly, rolling it up and bending the rolled cloth until it was pressed into as small a bundle as if it really was one of Christy's mom's kerchiefs.

"That's not possible," Christy signed. Danny just smiled and shrugged before stuffing it into his pack. He looked at the doorway opposite from the one they'd entered through and said, "Let's find out what's through that door."

Christy nodded, and this time as they stepped through the door they weren't surprised when the lighting came on suddenly. This room was identical to the one they'd just left. Instead of the shimmering coats on hooks, on one wall there were lockers. At least they looked like school lockers. They could see the seams clearly, except these were set right into the wall and didn't have any handles to open them with. Danny went over to one of them. Running his hand up and down on the flat surface, he searched for any hidden catch or other mechanism that might open it but couldn't feel anything.

After watching Danny have no luck with them, Christy turned her attention to the opposite wall and saw a strip of metal at eye level. It ran the length of the entire wall, and as she touched it, she noticed small raised circles that seemed to correspond to the placement of the lockers on the opposite wall. She found the one opposite the locker that Danny was trying to open and pressed it. It didn't give beneath her finger, but a warm sensation radiated from it to her fingertip. As she pressed her finger to it, the circle suddenly grew too hot, and she jerked back her hand in surprise, causing the locker opposite to snap open. Danny stumbled back in surprise and tripped.

"Sorry," Christy said, grinning as she reached down to help him up.

Danny grinned back. "Nice work!" he said.

Pulling the door all the way open, they found an empty hook similar to the ones that the coats had hung on in the previous room. Stacked on the floor of the locker were thin rectangular panes of clear glass about the size of postcards. Christy picked up the top one and began turning it over in her hands as Danny grabbed the one below it.

"I wonder what these are. Are they just small panes of glass?" Danny asked, examining his from every angle. The edges were smooth and a bit rounded, and the pane no thicker than the tip of a pencil.

"I don't know," Christy replied, "but I don't think they're just panes of glass. They feel heavier than the glass I'm used to."

She stopped turning hers over in her hand, holding it in her palm with her fingers gripped around it. A moment later it began to glow, suddenly projecting a sharp beam of light that began to coalesce into images and sound. It was playing out a three-dimensional scene.

CHAPTER 14

"I want to go home," Brad said again as they rested behind the tangled bushes.

Cory shook his head. "We are going home, Brad."

"No, we're not," Brad stated.

"Yeah, we are. That's where bullethead here is taking us— to the portal that leads home."

"Christy and Danny aren't going home," Brad said. "They have to come with us. Why aren't they with us?"

Cory had a sick feeling in his stomach listening to Brad. He knew well the way Brad's mind worked.

"We aren't going home," Brad repeated.

"Yes we are, Brad. Clacker is taking us."

"Not Christy and Danny," Brad said, shaking his head.

Cory took a deep breath. He wanted to pull his hair out he was so frustrated. Though he had hoped otherwise, he now definitively knew that Brad's 'we' included Christy and Danny, and there was no way to extract them from Brad's collective group. He tried another argument.

"We're just going ahead, that's all. We're going to wait for Christy and Danny at this swamp that Clacker's taking us to."

Brad just kept shaking his head. "Christy and Danny aren't here. We aren't going home."

Cory closed his eyes and took another deep breath.

"Ok, Brad," Cory conceded. "We'll go back and find the others. But then that's it. I don't want to hear another word out of you. Ask Jiminy Cricket there to take us back."

Startled, Christy dropped the glass and the projection ended instantly. Danny stared down in awe at his own sheet of glass, trying to mimic what Christy had done with hers by resting it in his palm with his arm extended. After a few seconds, it began to project an image. Danny stood still while Christy walked around him to view the projection from different angles.

Although the image was small, the scene was of tall, thin buildings that corkscrewed and bent into complete right angles before twisting upwards again. The scale of the projection made it seem as if there were bees buzzing between the buildings, but upon closer inspection it became clear that they were really flying machines. Suddenly, the image changed and zoomed in while they watched it, until it showed a close-up of the street level where ancients were going about their daily routines. In an odd way, it reminded Christy of New York City at rush hour, with people crossing streets and vehicles rushing by or stopped in traffic. In the background, it sounded as if there was some sort of narration, but it was unintelligible to her.

While Danny continued to watch the scene coalesce and change in front of him, Christy tried each of the raised dots on the opposite wall, and all but two lockers popped open. When Danny finally put down his piece of glass, the projection ended. They peeked into each locker but found most of them empty. In one of them, however, they did find another stack of the projection glass and a couple of the beautiful blue coats.

Danny made a point of trying to get each sheet of glass they found to project, and though some did nothing, most did what they expected. However, one that Christy found did something entirely different. Instead of a three-dimensional projection, it turned from clear to cloudy white, and odd symbols raced across its surface.

Christy tapped Danny on the shoulder and he put down the scene he was holding.

Christy signed, "I think these are books, kind of like e-book readers or tablets, only more advanced, like holograms. These projections remind me of the Princess Leia scene in Star Wars."

Danny nodded his agreement. He took one in his hand and hit it against the open edge of one of the locker doors. Christy expected it to shatter, but instead it just gave off a metallic hum. Danny placed it on his cheek and held it there for quite a while.

"Wow! It's still vibrating," he said, finally putting it down.

Christy signed, "It looks like glass but sounds and feels like metal." Danny nodded. They were both smiling uncontrollably. Selecting several of them, they slipped the prizes into their backpacks.

"Let's see what's in the next room," Christy suggested.

But when they reached the end of the room, they found themselves stymied. From a distance, it looked as if there was an open doorway, but it turned out to be an illusion. It became clear when they were close enough to touch it that it was just a solid wall with ... the image of an opening on it? Christy slammed her hand against the solid surface, and then kicked it for good measure. Danny searched around it for a switch or button, but after several minutes of fruitless exploring, he gave up.

"I wish Rob was here to see this, I wonder if he could get us beyond it. He figured out the portal door puzzle," Christy said as she slid down to the floor. "I can't believe we can't go any further. It's not fair!"

Danny laughed as she pounded the smooth floor with her fist.

"I'm serious, Danny, we've come too far to be stopped now."

Danny shrugged and Christy realized he'd really just come along for the ride, or to help her if he could, but he had no real desire to find a way in like she had.

They sat there on the tunnel floor just outside of the first room they'd found. Christy was too upset and frustrated to climb the stairs back the way they'd come just yet. Danny sat silently next to her, letting her have her moment.

"There's nothing we can do here now," he said finally. "We should catch up with the others. If I know Cory, he will whine and complain and make them rest more than they should. Finding them shouldn't be too hard."

Christy laughed, coming out of her funk slightly. "I've been travelling with him, believe me, you don't know the half of it," she signed.

They both laughed at their own observations about Cory. After a few minutes of silence, Christy stood up. Extending a hand down to Danny, she said, "You're right, we should catch up, but we're not going to yet. I want to look out of every one of those observation platforms we passed before we found the steps down here. Maybe there's a way down from one of them."

Danny groaned but reached up and took the offered hand. Just as they were hefting their packs, they heard footsteps from the direction of the stairs, still off in the distance. Caught off guard, they both froze.

Along with the footsteps, they heard, "Slow down, Brad! We don't even know if they're down there."

"Cory? Brad?" Christy yelled.

"Walker?" Cory replied.

"Here. Keep coming!" Christy yelled back.

After several minutes Brad rounded the corner at a run. Christy expected him to stop when he reached her and Danny, but after a quick glance at her, he rushed by them and headed into the room beyond. Two seconds later, Cory and Clacker came around the corner.

"Where'd he go?" Cory gasped, sucking in breath.

Christy pointed ahead through the opening. "The second we hit the stairs, he bolted ahead," Cory blurted out, still catching his breath. He stood up about to run after him when Clacker grabbed his arm and began to sign.

"I think Clacker says he shouldn't go in there," Danny said, responding to Cory's obvious confusion. "Something about it will hurt him I think. Without Brad to interpret though, I'm really only guessing."

"Then he can stay here," Cory said.

Christy was about to say something but Cory was already running into the room. She shrugged and looked at Danny, who quickly signed to Clacker that they'd be back soon. Just as Christy and Danny went through the doorway into the second room, they heard a startled cry followed by a groan. On the smooth floor, just in front of the illusion of a doorway, Cory was sprawled on the ground holding his face in his hands as blood trickled through his fingers. He'd run straight into the wall.

Brad, on the other hand, wasn't anywhere to be seen. It was as if the room had just swallowed him up.

Jack eagerly awaited the arrival of his new acquaintance. The young ancient was clearly intrigued with Jack and spent many hours trying to talk with him, and to Jack's delighted surprise, the jailor did not seem to mind the visits. He mostly left Jack and gi-BuMaz to themselves, only occasionally eavesdropping, which Jack assumed was to make sure nothing traitorous was discussed.

Since the first visit by his young friend, Jack had asked both of his fellow captives as much as he could about any traditions or ceremonies or even superstitions of the young of their species. It couldn't hurt to cultivate sympathy from a free ancient.

When his new-found friend arrived, Jack greeted him and they settled into a comfortable conversation. "You must be close to your gi release ceremony," Jack said knowledgeably.

The youngster shook his head. "No, I'm next cycle, not this one."

Jack played up his surprise. "Really? You seem older. I would have guessed you would be this cycle, not next.

And were it not for you still having gi, I would have said you were last cycle."

gi-BuMaz stood up straighter, clearly proud of the comments by his friend from another world.

They talked for only a few minutes when gi-BuMaz started to leave.

"Is there something you must do today, my young friend?" Jack asked.

"Yes, with my father gone, I must handle many duties."

Jack realized he hadn't yet asked about the boy's family. "Where is your father?"

gi-BuMaz hesitated, looking embarrassed.

"Is he no longer alive?" Jack asked gently.

gi-BuMaz shook his head. "That is not it. He is alive." Then he fell quiet. Again, he seemed to be embarrassed.

"Can you not speak of something?" Jack prodded.

gi-BuMaz lowered his eyes but he replied, "My father put you here. He is TuMaz."

Jack did his best to hide his surprise and nodded. "I don't hold that against you. We are friends," he said.

CHAPTER 15

"Open the door, Walker," Cory said, his voice muffled by his hands as he held a cloth over his bloody nose. Danny was kneeling beside him, trying to get a good look at the damage that Cory's face-first plunge into the hard wall had done to his nose.

Christy was staring hard at the illusion of a doorway, her hands tracing over each inch of what should have been an edge but wasn't.

"Cory, I'm sorry about your nose, but I don't know how to open this. Clearly Brad figured it out, so it's possible, but I don't know what to do. We have to wait for him, I guess."

Cory tentatively removed the cloth from his nose. When blood didn't flow from it, he threw the cloth away and stood up.

"What do you mean, wait?" Cory asked.

"Go ahead, see if you can get in there," Christy replied, inviting him to try with an exaggerated sweep of her hand.

After pushing and tracing and prodding the doorway, Cory finally turned and looked around the room. Christy and Danny had left a few of the locker doors ajar. "Could Brad be hiding in one of those?" he asked, pointing.

"No." Christy shook her head. "They're way too narrow."

Danny sighed. "Come on," he said. "I'm going back to find Clacker."

Christy nodded, and Cory shrugged, and they followed him out.

Clacker and Danny signed with each other when the four of them were back near the bottom of the staircase.

"Clacker says that the ancients have devised many things to kill his race," Danny explained. "The noise outside, the wind to dry his joints, the water to protect the portals, the noise horns that many ancients carry, and then the invisible noise that freezes." Danny shook his head, confused. "I think that's what he's saying. In those rooms there's a noise that he can't hear but that can kill him. I guess he can sort of feel it in his arms and legs, so he knows not to get too close."

"Well I guess we can't hear it either," Christy said, "but it doesn't seem to affect us."

"I think he's just chicken," Cory said, butting in, "which is funny since he looks like a lobster or something."

Danny, who had been staring at Cory's lips, rolled his eyes before turning away to sign with Christy. "Let's wait here with Clacker for Brad to come back," he signed.

Christy watched as realization dawned on Cory that Danny had deliberately excluded him from the discussion. He grabbed Danny by the bicep and tried to spin him around, but Danny quickly wrenched his arms free and continued to ignore Cory. When Cory grabbed Danny again, Danny turned around and shoved him, causing him to stumble.

"Don't you ever call one of us chicken. Got it?" Danny said.

Christy quickly pushed between them with her hands outstretched as she saw Cory step forward with his eyes narrowed. Just when Christy thought she was going to get tackled, she heard Brad's voice.

"Aren't you going to come? I've been waiting for you," he said.

"Brad?" Christy asked. The three of them were stopped in their tracks as Brad came out of the doorway and stood there with his eyes roaming the floor, waiting for someone to say something.

"Waiting? Where?" Cory asked, exasperated.

Brad just pointed at the side wall, the wall that ran adjacent to the massive main room.

"Show us, Brad," Christy said, gently.

Brad turned and went back through the doorway, with the three other humans following him. Clacker had to stay where he was.

When Brad arrived in the room with the illusion of a doorway, he opened the closest locker to it by pressing the corresponding button on the opposite wall. Once the locker was open, he reached in and felt along the inside of the locker for a moment before removing his hand. When the locker shut on its own, he simply stepped through the doorway. There had been no sound or movement or any other sign to suggest that the doorway was no longer an impenetrable obstacle.

When Cory touched the doorway, it was again solid. Christy stepped over to the wall with the buttons and press the one Brad had just pressed. She and Danny had opened that locker earlier but when they saw it was empty, they hadn't explored with their hands inside it.

Now Christy groped inside where she'd seen Brad searching and she felt it too. There was a small round opening near the top of the locker, large enough to insert her finger. She hesitated for a moment, pretty sure she knew what she had to do because Brad had just done it, but she was leery anyway. Shrugging off her uneasiness, she inserted her finger into the hole.

She extended her other hand towards the doorway, and it met no resistance. The barrier was gone. Cory and Danny stepped through and Christy removed her finger, stepping through quickly to follow them.

◇ ◇ ◇

"Where do you think he's gone?" Cory asked. They had followed the corridor behind the door to the point they were at now, confronted by four open doorways and no sign of Brad.

Danny pointed to the doorway on the far right. "That looks as if it's the closest to the room we've been trying to reach. Brad did point as if he'd been in it."

Christy nodded, liking the logic and said, "It's as good as any of them."

Cory frowned. "Shouldn't one of us stay here in case Brad comes back, or is lost somewhere?"

Christy smiled. "Lost? I have a feeling we'd get lost long before Brad would. We should stick together. If we choose the wrong doorway, my guess is Brad will find us."

Danny grinned and nodded, and Cory shrugged, which Christy took as a unanimous 'yes' and she started off through the open doorway.

They found themselves in another well-lit corridor, which went on for only a few dozen steps before ending abruptly at a tall door. Christy tried yanking on the recessed handle, but the door didn't budge.

"Let's go try another opening," Cory said. "There's no way Brad would've gotten through this if we can't."

"Cory, where have you been?" Danny asked. "What makes you think Brad wouldn't be able to get through here? He's made us look silly so far. I bet he opened this without even breaking a sweat trying to figure out how."

Cory snorted. "He got lucky last time. If you two had explored enough, you would have found that hidden button."

Christy shook her head. She was about to respond when the tall door slowly opened.

"Told you so," Danny said, grinning as Brad stepped through the door to join them.

"Stay with us from now on," Cory yelled at him. "Don't run ahead."

Brad stood in front of Christy with his eyes on the floor. "I need you to help me," he said. "I can't open it by myself."

Christy frowned. "What can't you open?"

Brad didn't answer— he just turned and walked back through door, with the others following right behind.

All four of them walked through another narrow corridor for a few minutes till they hit another door. Brad went right up to it and placed his hand on a small square at chest height, which was a slightly different color than the rest of the door itself. A few seconds later the door slid open silently. Brad stepped through and the rest of them followed suit.

On the other side of the door, Christy said, "Brad, stop, wait for us." Brad stopped a few feet up ahead, but the others were too amazed to actually notice if he'd stopped or not because they'd finally entered the large room they'd only seen from high up. Here at ground level, it was many times more impressive. Room definitely wasn't the right word. It was much too impressive in size for that. Stadium was more like it, but even that was doing this massive enclosure an injustice.

Christy had once been to a football game with her dad at the Superdome in New Orleans. This was like stepping out onto the field there, only three times as tall and too many times larger for Christy to even guess how big it was. But this was no wide-open venue like the Superdome had been.

This massive structure held what could only be described as an indoor city. It was filled with corridors and pathways and what looked like glass enclosures and walls and doorways and windows trailing up and up to the ceiling and off ahead, disappearing into darkness. Countless machines, all emitting a soft greenish glow from thousands upon thousands of tiny lights, and softly whirring, added to the eerie scene.

The impressive display trailed off into the distance in every direction. Adding to the impression of a city was the fact that at spaced intervals along the innumerable pathways snaking between the machines were actual lampposts with lights dimly shining as if turned down for a sleep period. Despite the lights, the overall impression was still of darkness as they'd noted from above, like a city at sleep. But from down here up close, they could see clearly enough to choose to explore if they wanted to.

"Hurry!" Brad finally said and trotted off ahead.

Christy shook her head, pulled out of her amazed stupor by Brad's command.

"Wait up," she yelled, taking off after him. Danny and Cory followed right behind her.

Brad darted left and right around free-standing machines and through a covered walkway. Christy and the others were too occupied trying to keep up with Brad to really notice or wonder what they were rushing past.

Just as Christy lost sight of Brad around a corner and started to panic, she turned the corner too and nearly bumped into him. He had stopped and was standing motionless in front of a door, which was partially opened a few inches. But Brad wasn't looking at the door. He was gazing up above the door, mesmerized.

Above the door was a symbol recessed into the wall. The symbol swirled and glowed with light in a rainbow of colors. After a few seconds of watching, it became clear that it was following a repeating pattern.

Christy watched as the sign hypnotized Brad. Finally, she shook him by the shoulder. He didn't even recoil from her touch; it simply brought him out of his trance. He stepped forward, grabbed the edge of the partially opened doorway and tried to force it open.

Christy grabbed a hold of the door edge to help him, intrigued and curious to get inside now. She had just enough space to get her hands onto the edge and help pull it open. But even though it gave a little more, it still wouldn't open enough to get through. Brad stepped back a bit and put his hands over his ears, rocking slightly and looking at Christy as she continued to tug on the doorway. Danny and Cory came up, and seeing what was going on, positioned themselves to also grab the edge of the door and help out.

Christy stopped them with a gesture of her hand and turned towards Brad, still rocking with his hands cupping his ears.

"Brad, what's hurting your ears? And why do you want to get in here? What's in here?"

Brad kept his hands over his ears, so Christy tried to pull them away, but he resisted her efforts. Finally, she tugged on his shirt and led him away a few steps from the jammed doorway. She tried again, and he let her pull his hands away.

"The singing hurts my ears," he said.

"Singing? Who is singing??" Christy asked.

Brad ignored her, stepped to the doorway, and resumed his tugging. When Christy came up behind him, she noticed the faint sound filtering out of the narrow opening. Christy frowned. The sound didn't bother her, so she shrugged and joined in again tugging with Brad. When Danny and Cory also joined in again, Christy stopped them momentarily and then counted to three, speaking and holding up her fingers. With them pulling together, the door slid open.

CHAPTER 16

Brad was right, Christy thought. The room they'd entered reminded her of some sort of shop or storage area, and it *was* singing. Or rather, the strange, shoebox-size devices were. On shelves around the perimeter of the room and on display tables in the center, the odd brass boxes were stacked neatly and polished to a brilliant shine. A quiet, melodic hum echoed in the air around them.

"Are they music boxes?" Christy wondered aloud. Intricate gears and dials were visible on the outsides of them, though most had smooth surfaces on top—well, somewhat smooth; myriad markings, dials, and knobs appeared to be etched right into the metal. As

Christy tried to take it all in, her attention came to rest on Brad.

Brad rocked on his heels with his hands over his ears. He was staring from one device to another, leaning closer to get a better look, seemingly intent on studying them. When the temptation to touch them seemed to become too great, he removed his backpack and took out his ear protectors, slipping them on before picking up the device closest to him, fiddling with it, and finally exchanging it for its neighbor. If any of them had a chance of figuring out what these things were, Christy knew Brad would be it. After a few minutes passed in awed silence, Danny turned to Christy. "Did you ever watch that special on TV about the two-thousand-year-old shipwreck they discovered in the Mediterranean?"

Christy shook her head.

"I've seen it a couple of times on the Discovery Channel. They found this brass device in it, with all these gears and small parts, and a few broken pieces of the outer surface of it, and there was enough of it still intact under the coral growing on it that they used this special x-ray technology and found out that the surface was etched with a chart of our solar system. They think it was used to calculate the movements of the planets and the moon ... even though it was at least a thousand years later before anything even close to that sophisticated was ever invented.

"These things all look like the recreation they made of what that device probably looked like before it spent two thousand years underwater."

"The etchings on some of these do kind of look like solar systems," Christy said. "Whatever these are, they must still work, or they wouldn't be humming like this."

Danny nodded. "I can feel them vibrating," he said, then added in a whisper, "Is that what's bothering Brad?" Christy nodded. She looked up to see Brad walking over to them with one of the devices in his hand.

"Can we go home?" he asked, pointing to the surface of the device in his hands. Danny gently took the device from Brad and set it down on the table. He examined it with rapt attention, proclaiming it to show the solar system that Earth belonged to and therefore be an exact replica of the shipwreck device, but Christy was more interested in inspecting as many of the others as she could before Brad's patience ran out. She tried to take in as many of them as she could, making mental maps of them as she perused the shelves.

"This is unbelievable!" she exclaimed. "There are dozens of solar systems here, and no two look the same. And there are some that seem to be maps rather than planetary systems."

Christy was first excited, and then annoyed. No one acknowledged her discovery— Danny was still focused on one of the devices and hadn't read her lips, Brad had his ear protectors on, and Cory was taking the opportunity to sit and rest. She sighed in frustration and was about to grab Danny's attention when he let out a gasp. He had one of the devices in his hands and as Christy joined him, he set it down on a table. "What does that look like?" he asked her.

Christy studied the shiny surface and its etched markings. She paused, uncertain why Danny was so excited, when all of a sudden it became clear.

"That's us! That's our portal, and the one in France." She was shocked it had taken her so long to recognize. There in front of her was a shockingly accurate outline of the coast of New England. Cape Cod was unmistakable, even though its shape was slightly different than she remembered from maps. The Atlantic Ocean and England and Western Europe were just as recognizable, once she'd realized what she was looking at.

She pointed first to one then to another small symbol etched into the surface. They were both filled with a dark orange color. "Those must be our portals we know about. I guess that means there's only those two on earth."

Danny read her lips and nodded. He placed his hand atop the device and frowned, checking a whole row of devices on the nearest shelf before turning again to Christy. "They've stopped vibrating," he said.

Christy stood still for a moment, listening. "You're right, Danny," she said. "The singing has stopped."

Just then Brad walked towards them with one of the devices in his hands. His ear protectors were slid down off of his ears.

Brad set the device down on the table next to where Christy and Danny were standing. "I turned them all off," he said. He pointed to the device he'd just put down and then to a corner of the room. There was a stack of crystals on the floor. Christy was surprised to see them there; perhaps she had been too enthralled by the brass devices to notice them. She picked one of the crystals up and realized it was just like the crystals in her grandfather's cave. She estimated that they were probably each about three inches long and an inch wide, all sharply faceted.

Suddenly, realization dawned on her. "Do these fit into the devices?" she asked Brad.

Brad put his ear protectors back on, took the crystal from Christy, and picked up the device he'd just set down. He reached inside the gears of the device with the crystal in hand, and when he pulled his hand away, the crystal was hidden in the device and the device was humming again.

"That's what Brad must have been doing this whole time ... taking the crystals out. He's amazing!"

Christy started to nod in agreement. "Why are you showing this one to us, Brad?" she asked.

Brad pointed to the surface etchings. "Rob told me about this," he said. "I drew it for him."

Danny leaned closer to the device to take a look. "Christy that looks like the mountain your grandfather told us about," he said.

When Christy looked closer, she noticed another one of the portal spots on the surface. "That's the portal island— it has to be," she said, pointing. "This may be a map of the whole Empty World. And look at the portal island. There's a small orange dot on it and another on the mainland and ..." She hesitated, then ran her finger along the surface just below the mountain with the hole through it. There were two more tiny orange dots.

"I think those orange colored dots are the four portals here that correspond to our two portals on earth. And they've color coded them the same as they colored the two portals on the device with earth etched on it." There were also other dots in many different colors on the Empty World etching. "I bet you these dots correspond to dots on the other devices here. And I bet you that means this world has portals on a lot of different worlds, not only Earth."

Danny inspected one of the devices on the table next to him: two blue dots, which matched the blue dot he'd seen on another solar system device. Sure enough, there they were on the Empty World map device. Christy watched as he seemed to confirm her observation. "This must be the master device that coordinates all the portals," Danny said, hefting the Empty World map device.

"But why?" Christy asked. "What are these for? If they only needed maps, why create these things? What do they do? Brad figured out how to turn off the power, but what is the power in them used for?"

Christy asked the questions without expecting answers and all she got was a shrug from Danny and a disinterested stare from Brad. Remembering colors that she didn't see on the Empty World device, Christy searched and found three devices that didn't seem to match up to anything.

"What do you think these are for?" she asked Danny.

"Don't know, but the etchings on these three are identical to each other. They look a little like solar systems, except they're only a bunch of circles with nothing on them. But maybe those are suns in the center."

Brad tapped Christy on the shoulder, and when she turned around to face him, he handed her one of the devices. It had collapsed into itself and was now barely half an inch thick, no longer shoebox size. Christy eyes widened as she took the device from Brad and turned it over in her hands. The surface still looked as if it were the same size, and the gears were still visible when she looked at it on edge, but somehow Brad had found a way to flatten it.

"Can you restore this, make it big again?" she asked Brad, handing it back to him.

He smiled and took it, searching with his finger on the bottom surface for a couple of seconds before the device sprang back to its original shape. Christy turned and grabbed the Empty World device, the Earth portal device, the Earth solar system device, and one of the three identical ones without any planets, and handed them to Brad to collapse.

"These ones all have something to do with Earth in some way, except the one that doesn't seem to be tied to anything. I think we should take them with us. Someone back home might be able to figure out what they are. They're a little heavy but now that they're collapsed we can fit them into our backpacks."

She handed one to Danny and Brad, and after a little protest from Cory, he took one too. She took the last one herself. Almost as an afterthought, she scooped up a few crystals and handed two to each of them.

"We should go collect Clacker and get out of here," Danny said finally. "We have to head to the swamp before the ancients catch up with us."

Christy nodded. "I hate to leave this place unexplored but you're right," she said. "We need to go."

Just then Brad held out his hand and said, "I want to take these too."

He was holding what looked like small silver soap dishes stacked together. They gleamed under the odd lighting of the room.

"What are they, Brad?" Christy asked.

Brad just stared at her and said again, "I want to take these, too."

CHAPTER 17

They'd been walking slowly through a corridor
with what looked almost like shops or dwellings
on either side when Danny pointed up above a doorway
they were approaching.

"That symbol is exactly like the one above the room
we just left," he said.

It was true. Above the doorway in front of them was
an identical symbol to the one above the device room,
and it too was swirling and glowing.

"None of the other rooms have had that symbol on
them. At least not any that we've passed," he added.

"Well, let's try to open the door and see what's
inside," Christy suggested. "The other room was worth

a look. With the same symbol, maybe this one will be too. Maybe Brad can open it."

Taking the cue, Brad stepped to the door and easily slid it open.

Brad entered first, with Danny and Christy following close behind. Cory shook his head. He had been grumbling since they'd left the device room about his pack being heavy and him being hungry, but with no choice but to follow them, he reluctantly went inside too.

The room was a low-ceilinged square enclosure, very different from the device room. This room also had table-like structure in its center, but its sides appeared to be made of a dark metal, and the surface was anything but flat. It was an amazing array of moving parts and swirling colors, and whatever it was doing, it was doing it almost too fast for the eye to follow. After watching it for a while, Christy determined that the cylindrical knobs on its surface moved up, flashed various colors, and then moved down again rapidly. The second they recessed into the flat surface, the colors shut off. Each of the glowing knobs looked about the same size as one another, slightly smaller than an average doorknob on Earth. Brad stood in front of the display, seemingly studying it.

"Great, we'll never leave now," Cory said. "Once he gets a look at flashing lights, he's good for hours at a time."

Christy ignored his comment. "I wonder what it is," she said.

Just then, Brad spread his feet wider apart and leaned over the display with his hands poised above the moving knobs.

Christy watched in fascination as Brad tried to hit each rising knob with his palms. The knobs were too fast for him, but he managed to hit them occasionally. After each successful hit, the display would pause for a second then start back up at the same particular knob, as if cycling back to its beginning.

Brad quickly caught on to the pattern, and when he successfully hit a random knob, he was able to hit the beginning one right as it started up again too. Soon the knobs had picked up so much speed that hitting them became impossible, and Brad gave up.

Christy chuckled. "It's like that arcade game." Cory, who had been slumped on the floor ignoring his brother and the rest of them, got up.

"Yeah, we both love Whack-A-Mole. I'm better at it than Brad though, which always bothered him, so my mom would force me to let him win." He thought for a second then frowned and added, "I got sick of it after a while, always having to let him win."

Christy didn't know why but his admission made her want to reach out to him to give his arm a friendly squeeze, but he turned away, finding a spot in the corner to slump back down before she was able to.

"I think this is exactly what we're joking about it looking like," Danny said.

"What do you mean?" Christy asked.

"Whoever made all this must have had a reason for putting this thing here.

Unless we've actually stumbled onto an arcade. The only other room with the matching symbol over its door has all those devices though, and I don't think they're games or toys."

"But you just said this could be an arcade game," Christy said.

"No, I don't mean it's a game per se ... but maybe it's like an elaborate lock. Remember how the portal has those carved blocks that need to be put in the correct order before the doorway will open? What if this is just another sequence that has to be followed and it will like open up a doorway when it is done correctly?

"This is the only thing in this room. Even the walls are bare. If this really was some sort of entertainment, there would be something else in here, I'd think, wouldn't you?"

Christy nodded slowly. "You could be right, but we don't have time to figure out what it does, unfortunately."

Brad had stepped back to the table and was trying again, and she watched him for a minute, almost hopeful that he'd prove her wrong. When he didn't succeed, she tapped him on the shoulder and said, "Come on, Brad, let's go."

This time Brad did react, pulling sharply away from Christy's touch and focusing on the display in front of him. Cory had been trying to rest, but when he heard Christy trying to get Brad's attention, he stood.

"I could solve that," Cory said. "I'm much faster than Brad with my hands." Though he looked as if he wanted to try, the temptation of leaving was much stronger. "Brad! We have to leave … Now!" he yelled.

Cory's voice must have gotten through to him, because he turned and picked up his pack and joined Christy and Danny.

Just then, Christy had an idea. "Cory, does that camera of yours take videos too?"

"Of course it does. Why?"

"Take a few seconds of video of this, will you?" she asked. "I promise I won't smash your camera," she added.

Cory stood up and eagerly did as she asked, then stowed the camera back in his pack, shouldering it with a grunt. It was time to get out of there.

The group had put miles between them and the amazing discoveries they'd made inside of the hill, but Christy couldn't help but continue to speculate.

"That place is the center of everything that's going on here, I just know it," she said aloud. They were in a protected area, so she had her ear protectors looped around the back of her neck. "I'm even more convinced of it since we actually saw some of what's in there. I know the sound must somehow be connected to it, probably the wind too. I wish we'd been able to explore more of it. Clacker calls it the 'power of the land' for a reason. He's still upset that he couldn't get inside anywhere with us."

Cory interrupted. "Bugman said something about taking us to his friends, didn't he?" he asked.

Christy tapped Danny and repeated Cory's question, and Danny nodded. "Clacker said he wanted to find his friends to help us but that we had to cross something he called the 'fire that rises from the ground.' I think he changed his mind once we met you guys though. Now he has just pretty much followed along with us."

"Brad should ask him," Christy said decisively, stopping and motioning for everyone to form a circle around her. She turned to Brad and gently touched his sleeve. He was getting less reactive to it and actually looked her in the eye for a second. "Brad, can you ask Clacker where he wants us to go. Does he still want to find his friends to help us?"

Brad started making a clicking noise in his throat and gestured with his hands, and Clacker eagerly responded.

It took Clacker touching Brad's chest gently before the boy answered.

"Clacker says he thinks we don't have time to search for his friends or to attempt to cross the fire and that we should keep on the path that we're on," Brad said.

Danny said, "I didn't like the sound of that place, the fire that comes from the ground. I'm kinda glad Clacker has changed his mind."

Christy nodded and started along the spongy moss path again and the rest of them followed.

"Danny," Christy said, making sure he was reading her lips. "Remember when we were overlooking the glider clearing, watching for anyone who might be guarding it?"

Danny nodded. "Yeah. What about it?"

"We never explored around that area for the path to the village. The village can't be far from there. That's where my grandfather must be."

As soon as Christy said that, Cory, who had only been half listening to the conversation, stopped short. "No you don't, Walker!" he shouted. "We're going straight to the portal, not off on some wild goose chase for your grandfather who's probably dead anyway."

Danny, who'd turned to look at Cory when he saw Christy do the same, caught most of what Cory had said. "Christy, I hate to agree with him, but he's right," he said. "You know you can't separate from us, there's only one glider. You'll never get across to the portal if you try to find the village while the rest of us use the glider."

Christy took a deep breath and signed and spoke at once. "I don't know what I'll do, but I know this—there's another way across. The ancients followed us with a boat after we'd taken the glider to the island, so there is a way to get across without it. I am responsible for getting you guys to the portal, so I'm going to do that, but I want to search for my grandfather too, so I may decide to hunt for the village after."

"It's out of your hands, Walker. I didn't tell you why we came back for you when we found you inside that hill. It was because Brad won't go home without all of us going. I couldn't get him to head towards the portal with me and Clacker when you and Danny went off in the other direction. He said that 'we' had to go home, and his 'we' included you two, meaning there was no going on without you. Your cute speech about being responsible for us getting to the portal doesn't mean a thing really, because Brad will flatly refuse to go if you traipse off in another direction. Without you coming too, we can't get there, period."

Danny signed a few words to Clacker who bowed his head in response. "Cory's telling the truth," Danny confirmed.

Christy didn't know how to respond, so she stayed silent as she started walking again. Soon they came into a severe sound area and had to put their ear protection back on. While they walked, Christy tried to figure out a solution; if Brad really wouldn't go without all of them being there, it was going to be tough. And she hated to admit it, but that meant that Cory was right, and would probably get his way.

CHAPTER 18

"I'll go on ahead and make sure the coast is clear," Danny signed to the group. They were gathered just short of the swamp. Christy motioned to the others, including Clacker, to wait until Danny came back. Danny headed off around the boulder outcropping that hid the Orator's old hut and the swamp beyond.

When he came back, he was grinning.

"What?" Christy signed.

Danny said, "I was just thinking about when your grandfather went ahead to check around the swamp. When he came back he had two pistols in his hands, and we hadn't known about them til then." Danny's grin turned to a frown. "I didn't take seriously just how dangerous your grandfather thought this world could be until that moment," he said.

Christy squeezed Danny's arm and nodded. "I remember that moment too."

As they moved out from behind the boulder outcropping and gathered next to the weedy shore of the swamp, Danny got right to work inspecting the boats. Unlike when they were there the year before, the boats were grouped close to the hut, not hidden further along the shore.

Danny threw his backpack in one and motioned for Clacker to help him push the boat until it was just beginning to float. "We can't tie the boats together," Danny said, "so I think Clacker and I should take Brad, and Cory should go with you."

"Ok," Christy replied. "The good news is that the wind does a lot of the work for us. I'll help put the other boat in." She stepped behind the second boat, and Danny helped get it in the water.

"Let's go," Christy said. "Cory, throw your pack in this boat with mine. Brad put your pack in the other boat with Danny's."

Cory did as he was instructed and turned to his brother. "Brad, come on."

Brad was standing a few feet away and ignoring the activity around him. Cory went over to him and gave him a small push to get him towards the boats, but Brad whined and spun around away from his brother, then stepped back a few feet. He hung his head and folded his arms around himself.

"No, no, no, no."

"What's wrong, Brad?" Christy asked gently. "We need to get in the boats."

Brad just stood there rocking and repeating 'no' whenever anyone tried to touch him.

Cory tried pulling him forward, but Brad screamed and pushed his brother away again. "No, no water, no water."

Christy turned to Cory. "Is he afraid of water?" she asked.

Cory shrugged. "We've never been on a boat before, so I don't know. But it sure looks like he has no intention of getting in one of these boats."

Danny, Cory and Christy all took turns trying to calm Brad down and get him in the boat, but he kept rocking and hugging himself, all the while mumbling, "No water, no water."

"Now what do we do?" Christy asked.

"We're stuck here," Danny said, looking at Brad. "Cory's right. It doesn't look like he's getting in that boat for anything."

They were stymied and frustrated. No matter what Cory used for an argument, Brad just stood apart, whining silently. Cory finally shook his head and left Brad alone. He moved over and stood next to Christy and Danny. "Can we go around?" he asked, glancing back at his brother.

Christy hesitated. "I don't know, but neither Danny nor I know the way if we try that. Plus, we're crossing the shorter width. It's much wider in either direction if we try to go around on foot. That's why my grandfather had us cross it. Even if we knew the way, it would take a lot longer to get to the portal."

Clacker, who had seen Brad's behavior, began to sign and pantomime to the group. Danny nodded along, while Cory just shook his head in bewilderment. Christy's understanding was somewhere in between the two.

Acting as translator, Danny said, "Clacker says he sees Brad is not willing to enter a boat. He says that to go around would mean we'd have to cross through the 'fire that rises from the ground,' and he says that is too dangerous. It would be foolish to try. He says the only way is by boat."

"What did he say about me?" Christy asked. "He pointed to me."

Danny nodded. "I think he said that you should go and get into the boat and leave."

"Why?" she asked.

"I'm not sure," Danny replied. "We could ask Brad to translate for us if he wasn't so upset."

Cory was listening and spoke up. "Just get into the boat, will you, Walker? In case you haven't noticed, Brad has a thing for you. Even the bu— even Clacker has noticed it."

"What if it doesn't work?" she asked. Danny started to say something when Cory interrupted.

"I'll stay with him until he decides to follow you."

Clacker waved for attention, then signed and pointed to himself.

Danny translated. "Clacker's going to stay too, so the three of you will share the boat."

"Oh, great. That will be fun," Cory said.

Christy and Danny were letting the wind take them across the swamp. Neither of them wanted to hasten the boat along by paddling, so the paddles just sat in the bottom, untouched. They were almost out of sight of the shore, and there was still no sign of the other boat following. Finally, Danny picked up his paddle as they bobbed towards one of the triangle shaped tree stumps and used it to stop them against it. Odd silver insects that were perched there opened their parachute-like wings and shot off with the wind.

With some effort, the two of them were able to keep the boat from moving forward. They didn't have to sign or speak. Both of them knew the plan was to stay put until the other boat came along ... if it came along.

After several minutes passed, the effort to keep the boat in place while the wind battered against them was wearing on Christy and Danny. Twice they broke free from the stump they had latched onto and were forced to grab the next one further along.

Christy finally wedged her paddle into a hole in one of the stumps that granted them a reprieve from their struggle.

"Danny, what if I made a mistake?" she asked. Danny was turned sideways to face her, so she knew he could read her lips. "What if I'm just being selfish? If he's not going to get into the boat, maybe we should have tried to go around the swamp."

Danny waved her concerns away. "Clacker said we couldn't have gone around, even if we wanted to. I didn't like the sound of whatever the 'fire that rises from the ground' is, did you?"

Christy shook her head. Alleviated temporarily from her doubt, she resumed her silence. Just when Christy was about to ask if they should think about giving up and just let the wind push them across the swamp, she saw a boat approaching from behind them, bobbing and swaying with the wind. It seemed Cory and Clacker had succeeded in getting Brad into the boat.

CHAPTER 19

Once Brad had gotten in the boat, it had caught up to Christy and Danny's boat quickly, and the wind pushed them swiftly across the swamp.

"Let's leave the boats here with the others," Christy said as they slid towards the shore. "We need to hurry. Be on the lookout for any trouble."

Cory was splashing in the shallow water, not waiting for Clacker to pull the boat into the reeds. Brad was still sitting in the boat with his head down and his arms wrapped around his head.

"Come on, Brad, get out of the boat," Cory yelled. "We've made it across and we have to get going." Cory waited and when Brad didn't get out or even acknowledge Cory's attempts to get him out of the boat, Cory threw up his hands, stormed off and sat down a few yards away.

Danny jumped into the water and helped Clacker slide the boat with Brad still in it into the reeds. Then he tapped Brad on the shoulder, gently took him by the elbow and tugged until Brad stood up and stepped onto shore.

Christy motioned all of them to gather around her. She called to Cory who was sitting pouting at Brad's stubbornness, and he finally got up and came over.

"After we head to the glider, we'll try to find the village. It has to be nearby."

"No we're not, Walker. Forget it. We get the glider and head home," Cory said.

"I'm not leaving until I know what's happened to my grandfather, even if I have to find him by myself," she replied.

"We can't let you, Walker. Remember, Brad won't go anywhere if we all aren't together. Even Danny agrees with me on this one, don't you kid?"

Christy glanced at Danny who had read Cory's lips. As Danny shrugged, looked sheepishly at her, and then nodded, Christy began to tear up. Clacker, who appeared to be getting very good at gauging the emotions of his young companions, stepped up and raised his arms. After clicking furiously for a few seconds, he tapped Brad, who responded with a long series of his own clicking. Clacker nodded and began signing and clicking again. When he was done, he touched Christy on the shoulder as gently as he could.

"Brad, can you tell us what Clacker just said?" Danny asked.

Brad just stood there silently.

"Brad? We need you to tell us," Christy pleaded.

Brad lifted his eyes finally. "He says he knows Christy wants to find her grandfather, but he doesn't want us to delay any longer. He's really afraid that we're either being followed by the group that captured us, or that somehow that group will head us off before we get to the glider. He says he'll go find Jack while we cross in the glider."

Christy sighed. It wasn't ideal, but it seemed her only choice. She nodded her thanks to Clacker, who bowed slightly to her in response. "Let's go. We're not far now," she said. "I'll lead. Danny, you walk in the back. Cory, try to keep an eye on Brad, please."

They shouldered their packs and walked away from the boats, leaving the swamp behind.

Christy and Danny were leading. They'd followed the same route the year before with Christy's grandfather, so they knew the way. Clacker kept guard in the back of their procession, silent and alert.

They decided to head to the tunnel where they'd met the Orator the year before. It would be in a brutal sound area, but Christy anticipated that they'd need a rest and hoped the Orator might be there with some news for them. They trudged on across the rolling landscape, fighting against the strength-sapping moss that quivered underfoot. It was no different from the moss they'd been enduring the whole way, but after effortlessly crossing the swamp, it was particularly depressing to encounter again.

After trekking several arduous miles through the moss, Christy signaled them all to put on their ear protectors. She recognized the area. A stand of wind altered trees loomed ahead and just beyond it the boulder outcropping of the Orator's tunnel.

Once upon it, they found the entrance to the tunnel immediately, and kept walking with their ear protectors on until they'd gotten far enough inside to know the sound had lessened. Cory took his off and threw his pack down. He pointed to Danny's ear protectors. "Why do you wear those?" he asked. "You don't need them."

"The pressure without them is annoying. It's more comfortable for me to wear them than endure the pressure for long stretches of time. It makes my head throb," Danny replied.

Cory didn't bother to acknowledge Danny's answer. Rather, he dug into his backpack and started chewing on some of the dried meat.

Christy just shook her head. Cory's manners left much to be desired.

"Is there any water in here?" Cory asked.

"There's a small stream just outside the entrance. We'll all fill up when we leave," Christy said.

"I need some now," Cory said.

"Then go, don't forget to put on the ear protectors, though," she said, and then slumped down beside Danny and Brad. Clacker stood slightly apart, keeping a watchful eye as always.

Cory got up, pulled out his ear protectors and his water bottle and stalked off toward the entrance. A few seconds after he disappeared around the bend and out of sight, a blood curdling scream startled the group from their rest.

"Has your father returned yet?" Jack asked gi-BuMaz. The young Ancient was visiting every day now.

gi-BuMaz lowered his eyes for a moment. "Yes, and I have to be careful. If he knows I'm here, I will be in trouble."

Jack noticed the hesitation and realized that gi-BuMaz was hiding something in his response.

"I'm sorry, my friend. You should probably leave here. But is there something else you wanted to tell me?"

gi-BuMaz shook his head. "No." Then he blurted out, "Yes. The Cleaner and four young humans have been captured and are on their way here. My father was leading a group of sies but came back early. He now waits for their arrival."

Jack slumped back against the cold stone wall behind him. Fear and anger gripped him. He took a deep breath to steady himself, moved toward the door again, and motioned for gi-BuMaz to move closer.

Jack spoke in a conspiratorial whisper. "I don't want you to get in trouble but before you go, can you tell me anything about the four young humans on their way here?"

gi-BuMaz nodded, looked behind him quickly then said, "My father boasted that when they arrived, you would not be happy. He said you would know two of them. One is a female and one needs no protection from the sound. But he was also confused about something. He said that two of the humans were the same. Do you know what he meant by that?"

Jack was reeling— Christy and Danny were back. He had to think.

"No gi-BuMaz, I am not sure what he meant by that. You must go now before your father knows you are here." Then he said, "And thank you for telling me."

gi-BuMaz nodded and turned, disappearing back the way he'd come.

Jack had to find a way out. And what did TuMaz mean when he told gi-BuMaz that two humans were the same? They looked the same? Suddenly it hit him. The Peters twins ... it had to be. He'd never seen or heard of twins amongst the ancients. Two humans looking exactly the same would be upsetting to them. The echoes of gi-BuMaz's footsteps had barely dissipated when Jack realized something else. His young friend had also said that his father had come back early. Why would TuMaz come back ahead of his prisoners? What did he have to do?

CHAPTER 20

Jack was dozing off in the midday heat, as he did every day. Unless they put him to work at the shrine, he had nothing else to do. Today he was startled awake by the sound of commotion down the hall. Before he could even wipe the sleep from his eyes, TuMaz's face was pressed into the opening of his cell door.

"Do you understand me?" the ancient asked.

Jack nodded and replied, "Yes, you smelly goat, your betters here have taught me well, including insults to throw at you. Want to hear them?"

TuMaz didn't take the bait; he just snorted to show his distain and said, "I have news of your friends."

Jack knew what was coming, but he said, "Why should I believe anything you say to me?"

"Because I am not lying. Your friend the Cleaner and four of your young have been caught and are being brought to me."

Jack turned away, burying his face in his hands. He hoped he was reacting as if it were unexpected and unwanted information.

TuMaz continued. "I will throw them in prison with you when they arrive." Grinning viciously, he turned and left without waiting for a response.

Christy couldn't believe their bad luck. Cory had walked right into two waiting Ancients who'd been just as surprised by him but had taken advantage of their good fortune by grabbing the boy and letting him continue screaming till the others rounded the bend. The two ancients guarding the crestfallen group stood apart, silently and vigilantly ensuring that nobody escaped. Christy wiped the tears away and saw that Danny and Cory were doing the same. Brad just sat quietly next to his brother. They had been granted a short rest.

They'd been surrounded and subdued quickly once Clacker had been incapacitated with a short blast and his arms secured with rope. The blast had also hurt the humans' ears— all except Danny's— but it was not nearly as powerful as the sound zones they constantly encountered, so their ears were ringing, but not badly injured.

Danny whispered to Christy that he'd named the two guarding them: Bearded Ancient and Smelly Ancient. Under different circumstances she'd have had a chuckle over the names, but she didn't feel like laughing at anything while under guard by two ancients.

After coming out of his blast-induced paralysis, Clacker stood up and endured in silence as he usually did, only occasionally clicking slowly as if he were snoring quietly. Christy had no idea if he actually did snore, or even if he really slept, since she had not witnessed it in days of travelling together.

The only real mercy granted to them was that they'd been allowed to keep their packs, which the ancients must have considered harmless. Both of the ancients guarding them carried the menacing spears that Christy knew so well. Cory hadn't seen one until he'd turned the corner in the tunnel and was confronted with a whole group of ancients pointing their spears at him. His screams had lured the rest of them right to their waiting captors and into their present situation.

Christy finally chanced to speak to Danny, Cory, and Brad, refraining from signing since she knew that the ancients all had knowledge of a modified version of American Sign Language. They'd picked it up years and years ago from other humans who'd crossed over. Seeing the benefit to the hand language, it had spread rapidly throughout the Empty World between the various groups and villages of ancients, according to her grandfather. She tapped Danny to get his attention first, then began to speak.

"I'm so sorry. I don't know what's in store for us now, and I feel responsible for this all," she said between sniffles.

"It's not your fault we're here, and you know that," Danny argued. "It's nobody's fault, really. I couldn't let Brad come to this world alone when I saw him jump, and you and Cory couldn't help but come after Brad and me. That's all. Nobody's fault," Danny said again. He squeezed Christy's arm in support.

Danny glanced at the two ancients, who were ignoring them.

"Why don't we ask them what we're doing here?" Danny said, also intentionally not signing. "They don't look like they're angry with us. They just seem to be standing guard. I'd like to know why Angry Ancient left in such a hurry with the rest of them."

Christy nodded, and Danny stood up, catching the attention of both ancients. Bearded Ancient grunted something, waving his spear. Danny signed and the other one rested his spear by his side.

Shorty Ancient answered by signing, "We don't question our leader. Why he needed to hurry back to our village is none of our concern. Our job is to bring you."

"Well," Christy began, "if they're taking us to the village, maybe I'll see my grandfather there."

Danny nodded. Suddenly, Brad spoke up. "No, we're going home soon."

Cory stirred out of his fear- and exhaustion-induced stupor. "No we're not, Brad," he said. "We're not going home anytime soon. We're probably going to die here."

Brad started to answer. "No, Cory we—"

"Shut up." Cory cut off his brother, his voice cracking with emotion. "I'm sick of you talking about going home. You're the one who got us into this." Cory wrapped his arms around his knees and began to sob loudly into them.

Christy tentatively placed a comforting hand on Cory's shoulder, which was shaking with his sobs. He didn't push her away, so she squeezed gently in sympathy.

"Maybe we can get out of this," she said.

Cory snorted as he'd done a thousand times before to show his disbelief, then went back to crying, his head buried in his arms, muffling his sobs.

Christy tried to start again, sounding more cheerful and positive than she really was. "I hate to bring this up, but when we escape again, if we become separated, each of us should continue on if we get the chance. Even if it's only some of us, ok?" Christy looked around to see if they'd understood what she was saying.

Nobody nodded or said anything to indicate they'd understood.

"Walker, I'm as tired of your bologna as I am of Brad's," Cory said. "Just shut up and realize we're not getting out of here." In the silence after Cory's outburst, they all could hear Clacker, his eyes shut, continuing to snore or whatever it was he was doing. Finally, Clacker's eyes opened and the clicking stopped.

Brad spoke then. "Cory, don't be upset. Clacker says, 'Cory has to remember the knife in his pack.'"

Cory picked his head up, sniffled and said, "Great. Clacker thinks we can overpower these guys with a pocketknife. Guess he doesn't see the spears they're carrying."

Brad continued as if he hadn't heard his brother. "Clacker says, 'the ancients are not as wary of me now that I've been tied up and they have in their ear plugs, so they have set down their bull horn.' Clacker says, 'we will get an opportunity to try for an escape but that it will be much more dangerous than before.'"

When Brad stopped talking, Christy asked, "Brad, what else has Clacker said?" She was pretty sure now that Clacker's snoring was in fact his quiet attempt to talk to Brad.

Clacker clicked, nodded his head down and up and clicked again. It must have been a prompt to Brad because he said, "Clacker says, 'I will tell you when to do what I plan. We must somehow table the turns on the Ancients.'"

Christy laughed at Brad's literal retelling of Clacker's badly mangled expression. She was becoming familiar with his way of recounting someone else's words as if that person were speaking. She imagined that Cory was so familiar with it by now that it just seemed normal to him.

Danny was watching and reading Brad's lips, and he grinned too.

"What? We're supposed to overpower these two and make them captives, and just walk out of here? The bug is delusional if he thinks that," Cory scoffed.

Clacker seemed to sense the resignation of his young companions and started to click rapidly. When he stopped and nobody said anything, he took a small step over to Brad and tapped him with his leg.

"Clacker says, 'one of you must cut my bonds so that I can defend you during our escape. Two others must pull the ear plugs of the ancients while we all wear our ear protectors. When we have done that, I am going to incapacitate them as they did to me. We have to imprison them somehow or they will alert the others and then we wouldn't be able to make it to the glider'."

"Oh, sure, piece of cake there, Shell head," Cory said, burying his face back into his arms.

"Brad, do you think you and Cory could cut Clacker's ropes and free him while Christy and I pull the earplugs out of the two ancients' ears?" Danny asked.

Clacker clicked furiously for a few seconds before Brad answered. "Clacker says 'Brad can do it but we need to wait till it is dark in here.'"

Christy and Danny both groaned. It never got dark in this tunnel. The eerie light was on constantly. Danny faced away from the two ancients and signed the bad news to Clacker.

CHAPTER 21

Clacker shook his head while talking directly to Brad. After he stopped, he tapped Brad again with his foot. Brad repeated what Clacker said, word for word. "If there is no darkness, then we must overpower them without that advantage. To that end I will do this." Brad stopped, and Clacker used his tied claws to make a snapping sound. He repeated it only stopping for Brad to retell his instructions. For once, Brad didn't need prompting.

He said, "When I signal those two snaps, Danny should be able to cut my bonds. Once freed, I will be able to use my sound advantage on our captors. But only if Cory and Christy have succeeded in pulling out the earplugs the ancients use to protect themselves. Do you all understand me?"

They all turned from Brad and nodded at Clacker, who took one step closer to the group seated on the ground. As soon as he did that, the two ancients grunted, pointed their spears and made it clear that they didn't want Clacker to go any closer to the humans.

Clacker disregarded the ancients and took another step towards the kids. Again, both ancients came towards Clacker, spears pointed at his midsection. The kids were waiting for Clacker's signal, but apparently, he'd changed the plan. Maybe it was the fact that their captors had gotten closer, and Clacker saw an opportunity.

All of a sudden, Clacker launched himself up and almost over the two ancients, his legs wide. At the last second, he thrust his legs inward in a scissoring motion, striking the two and forcing their heads into each other. They both collapsed in a heap, spears clanking on the hard ground of the tunnel.

Clacker landed awkwardly and sprawled out on top of both of the now unconscious ancients. As soon as Danny seemed to come out of the shock of what they'd just witnessed, he rummaged in Cory's backpack and pulled out the pocketknife. Danny pried open the knife and rushed to Clacker, sawing quickly through the rope tying his arms.

Clacker stood up. After momentarily checking the two incapacitated ancients, he took his own former bonds and tied them up with them, showing impressive dexterity with his claw-like hands. Everyone stared at him, surprised at the quick change of plans. Clacker looked at them all and instead of trying to speak through Brad, he did a very human thing: he shrugged. Christy couldn't help but laugh. Then Clacker started off, motioning for them all to follow. They were in escape mode again.

As soon as they broke into the fresh air, they stopped and gathered around Clacker. He clicked rapidly and touched Brad on the shoulder.

Brad said, "That worked better than I'd hoped. Thank you, Danny, for catching on quickly and cutting my bonds."

Danny smiled, and Clacker said something more, again prompting Brad to translate. "Those two ancients will be out for a long time and won't bother us. But we must keep going and move along quickly."

Jack was wavering between despair and denial about the kids and Clacker. He couldn't imagine how Christy could have gotten back. He knew she'd try to come and find him. That would be only natural for the girl and Jack had to smile at the thought of his granddaughter's determination. But Connie and Doug must have almost kept her under lock and key for the past year. CaTaz and PeSaz seemed upset about it as well. Having spent the last year with him in the small locked cell, they shared in his pain.

Loud yelling from the corridor brought Jack, CaTaz, and PeSaz to their feet. CaTaz's brother, NaTaz, came into view, and while rolling his eyes, unlocked their cell and opened it, motioning for the prisoners to step back. When they did, TuMaz stepped into view around the jailor, and entered their cell. "I need you two to come with me," he said. He pointed at his two former companions and nodded to NaTaz, who reluctantly grabbed CaTaz and PeSaz gruffly and led them out of the cell. TuMaz closed the cell behind them, leaving Jack as the only occupant.

"I have something of yours that I now know how to use," TuMaz said. He pulled out the gun, which he had wondered about for a year. "I think you had better tell your two companions it would not be wise to disobey me."

Jack nodded, resigned. "Do as this scum says. That," he said, pointing to the pistol in TuMaz' hand, "will kill you if he uses it on you."

Both of his cellmates nodded their understanding as NaTaz pulled them away. TuMaz-Tan waited behind until he and Jack were alone.

"You will rot in here until I return," TuMaz said, grinning. "And know this ... the small one and the female who traveled with you are on their way here, but you will not see them again before I send you to your death." Jack's eyes blazed with hatred for the ancient as he sprang up and thrust his head as far into the small opening as he could.

The suddenness and strength of Jack's anger startled the ancient, and he pulled back with fear in his eyes. Jack grinned viciously back at him and said, "I will kill you if I get the chance, so be on your guard. I'll find a way to live and if you harm the humans and the Cleaner, I will avenge them."

TuMaz was still too off balance to reply, so he turned and followed the two prisoners and NaTaz out.

An hour later, NaTaz crept back to the cell quietly and said, "Jack, I have to go. TuMaz wants me to go with him and CaTaz and PeSaz. I have left instructions for your new jailor to be kind to you." NaTaz looked around and then leaned in and whispered, "We're going to meet up with your young friends. TuMaz does not entirely trust those he left to guard them. He thinks everyone is incompetent. I hold no ill will towards you. In fact, I have come to admire you, so I will try to lessen any burden that TuMaz may place upon your young friends."

Jack was about to say something but NaTaz looked around nervously and held up his hand for silence. "I can't say more because I know nothing else."

"Thank you, NaTaz, it is very good of you," Jack said, choking up with emotion.

NaTaz nodded and smiled. Then he hesitated for a moment, as if weighing whether to say something else. Instead he thrust his hand quickly into the small window opening and dropped something into Jack's cell, then turned and left.

Jack bent down and picked up what NaTaz dropped. It was a small wooden key, delicately carved. Jack frowned at it. Wood? He knew that metal was not something the ancients currently knew how to work with but with metal artifacts strewn everywhere across the world, he figured they should have learned to melt it down and repurpose it by now.

The ancients certainly did use what metal they could find a purpose for. The prison Jack was in, although made of wooden walls and a wooden door, had a metal lock that was opened by what must have been a very old, metal skeleton key. Perhaps this wooden key was NaTaz's attempt to copy the key to his jail cell. Jack gently tried to bend it and noted that it seemed to be made out of a strong wood. But would it be strong enough to actually work in the keyhole, or would it snap?

Jack was elated at his chance of escape, but simultaneously frightened to the core. He had a feeling he knew why TuMaz was not waiting, why he was going to meet the kids coming back to the village. And he was afraid it had something to do with that pistol. Jack got angrier by the minute as he thought of the ancient and what he might be planning.

Jack wanted to try the key right away, but he knew if he were fortunate enough to get the door open, his only chance of escape was waiting to leave under the cover of darkness.

The time inched by slowly. Jack had a short conversation with the new jailor when he brought food. The ancient actually seemed apologetic about keeping him in the cell. As the day wore on, Jack thought of the wooden key and smiled. At least the new jailor wouldn't have to apologize much longer, Jack hoped.

While Jack waited impatiently, gi-BuMaz paid him another visit. The youthful ancient stood in front of the small opening in the door and greeted Jack.

Jack frowned at him, hoping to get him to leave quickly, as the light was getting dimmer. "What brings you here today?" he asked curtly.

gi-BuMaz did not seem fazed by Jack's attitude.

"I have news of your friends," he said.

Jack forgot about the light, and about trying to get rid of the ancient. "What? Tell me, please."

gi-BuMaz said, "Your friends have escaped."

Jack grinned at the youth. "Tell me everything you know about it."

gi-BuMaz stood up just a little bit straighter. "My father came home very upset. It seems that your friends overpowered the two that my father tasked with bringing them back here."

Jack pumped his fist "Way to go, guys!" he said in English.

"What?"

"Nothing, my friend. Do you know anything else?"

"Just that my father has left the house and said he might be gone for a few days."

Jack made small talk for a few minutes, but soon made it clear that he wished to be left alone, so gi-BuMaz walked away.

When it was finally dark enough, Jack put the wooden key in the lock, and said a silent prayer that it would work. The key met resistance and Jack stopped turning. He was afraid that it would snap off in the keyhole, but knowing he had no choice but to keep turning until the outcome was determined, he tried again.

The resistance was steady, but Jack kept turning the key slowly until he thought he heard the lock disengage. The key snapped at the same time. His heart sank as he pulled out the stem of the wooden key, afraid it had broken too soon. Expecting the worst, he tried the door. It opened!

CHAPTER 22

Clacker pushed his human friends to keep walking. Their spirits were high. Even though they expected to be pursued, they felt the risk of the ancients catching up before they made it to the portal was small. Since leaving the tunnel they'd been forced to head in a more northerly direction, directly into the fierce wind. Christy remembered it—and how hard it made traveling—quite well.

She led them to the same spot to rest for the night that she, Danny, Rob and her grandfather had used the year before. It was in a well-protected area where they could take off their ear protection for the night. The next day, they'd only need their protection for a short while before the horrific sound abated for the rest of the way, though the wind would never let up.

Propped up against a warm boulder, not even facing any of her companions, Christy was enjoying the rest after fighting the wind all day. She was chewing on a strip of dried meat when Cory yelled, "Brad, what is that? What are you doing?"

Christy jumped up and turned. Brad ignored his brother, too occupied by the thin, glass projection plate he held in his hand. A scene of ancients in a small city or village was projecting up into the air about a foot above. Cory walked around his brother, marveling at the display. Christy saw the stack of the plates next to Brad just as Danny began to explain.

"I gave them to Brad a few minutes ago. I bet he watches them all," he said and signed. Christy smiled and rummaged through her pack for the ones she had taken with her and set them down next to Brad on top of the ones that Danny had given him.

After explaining to Cory where the plates had come from and watching Brad for a while longer, Christy sat back down against the boulder. It had been a long day, and she needed to take advantage of every minute they had to rest.

A few minutes later, Danny slid down next to her.

"After what we've seen him do, I bet if anyone can figure those things out, it will be Brad," he signed. Christy nodded and closed her eyes, smiling. Since the day was ending they decided to stay put for the night, and soon were settling down to sleep. Christy had already dozed off when she was suddenly startled alert by another gruff yell from Cory.

"Come on, Brad, settle down and get some sleep. Put those things away."

Brad was still holding one of the projection glass plates in his hands and watching, completely ignoring Cory. Danny, who was still next to Christy, tapped her in the dark to get her attention and leaned over to whisper in her ear.

"Brad has looked at each of those disks at least twice apiece, and the one he's looking at now, he's watched several times."

Brad was at least ten feet away from them and they couldn't tell what the projection was showing, but it was the only light source and gave off warmth like a campfire. Christy watched for a few minutes, but then sleep won the battle for her attention and she slid down, grateful for the soft moss beneath her. Later on in the night, she woke up and turned over to find Brad still sitting up, eerily illuminated by a projection playing out above his hand.

When Christy woke in the morning, Brad was sleeping peacefully, and Cory and Danny still seemed to be as well. Clacker, on the other hand, was standing a few feet away. She still wasn't sure that he ever slept. He always seemed to be standing there waiting for the rest of them to get going every day.

The square disks she and Danny had given Brad were nowhere to be seen. When she'd fallen asleep the night before, they'd been scattered at Brad's feet, on his lap, or in his hand. She opened her backpack and saw that he had put some back. She could almost bet that he'd given her back the same ones she'd given him and put the ones from Danny back in his pack too.

Before the others got up, Christy spent some time thinking. She even started to re-evaluate Cory's behavior since they'd all been thrust together. She wasn't ready to like him, but she felt she was maybe beginning to understand some of his anger, and why he always acted mean to everyone. She could see how it would be really hard always having to look out for someone else, never having time alone, and then being yelled at when you failed. Maybe she didn't like Cory, and she couldn't really see a time when she ever would, but she was beginning to feel sorry for him all the same.

"Do you think it's all there? I hope they repaired the damage from last year," Christy signed to Danny.

They were at the same vantage point they'd used the year before to scope out the clearing and the glider with her grandfather. Just as it had been the year before, the glider was resting on the massive slab of granite, but also like last year, the wings weren't visible. Christy imagined they were probably back in the hut, broken down into their pipe components. The wooden ramp was there and off to the side.

Danny nodded. "Why wouldn't it be?" he signed. "I don't think they'd put it back on the slab if it wasn't working. But we need to find out fast!"

Christy nodded and the two of them retreated from the overlook back to where they'd left the twins hidden with Clacker.

Even though Christy had warned them to be silent, Cory immediately started in complaining about being left behind, and how he wasn't going to take it anymore.

"Shut up!" Christy hissed. "For this to work, you have to cooperate. When we get to the clearing, Cory, you take Brad and stand by the glider, then wait for Danny and I to bring the wing tubing from one of the huts. Assembling the wings is real easy and once we've done that we can put the silver cloth over the framework. From there, we'll be ready to go."

Once she got nods from them all, even Brad, she motioned them forward and down to the clearing. The clearing was so exposed that the wind was even more of a hindrance than in almost any other area they'd been in. Without anything to break its force, it relentlessly pounded at them as they huddled next to the massive stone block of the launching ramp.

Christy beckoned Danny and they sprinted off to look for the wing piping and the metallic cloth covering. They found everything stacked neatly in the same hut they'd been in the previous year.

Christy grinned. "Score one for tradition, I guess."

Danny was gathering an armful of the tubing when he shouted, "Look!" He held one of Jack's pistols in his hand.

Christy came over and took it from him gingerly. "Maybe this is the one Rob was given. He must have dropped it as we were taking off."

"It has to be. Where else would it have gone? It never made it to the island, as far as we know."

Christy just nodded and handed it back to him. He started to shake his head no, but realizing she wasn't going to keep it, he took it and tucked it under his belt, hidden beneath his sweatshirt. They continued to gather the piping in silence.

When they were back at the glider, Christy led the rest of the group in assembling it.

For once, whether it was because he sensed they were close to going home, or just because of Christy's urgency, Cory didn't argue. He went with Christy, Brad, and Clacker and began the arduous task of pushing the wooden ramp against the end of the stone launching pad.

When Danny had finished putting the glider wings in place, he joined them. The heavy wooden ramp resisted every inch of their effort, its crude wheels barely doing the job they were so poorly designed for. Christy couldn't believe that a culture as advanced as the one that'd built the strange city they'd found could regress so badly.

After the ramp was in place, Christy slumped down against the stone slab and rested alongside the others, all of whom, except Clacker, had also slipped down into sitting positions, gratefully taking a few minutes to rest.

Getting Brad's attention, Christy said, "Can you tell Clacker that we will need him to push us once we set the cloth over the glider wings and get set in our seats? I think he probably knows already what's going to happen, but just in case."

Brad and Clacker spoke at length, Clacker's voice clicking and vibrating as he waved his clawed hands and pointed back the way they'd come. When he was done, he tapped Brad who began to translate for them.

"I will do as you say. I will also go to find your grandfather, Christy, he who is my friend, Jack. I wish you all well and hope we meet again someday."

Christy had tears in her eyes as she hugged him. It caught Clacker by surprise, but he stood there and accepted it, clicking and humming something else until she let him go.

Christy asked, "What did he say, Brad?"

"I will miss you humans, too," he translated.

Danny, who had read Brad's lips, smiled and impulsively hugged the creature too.

"Yeah, thanks Bullethead, but I ain't hugging you for nothing," Cory chimed in.

At that, Christy and Danny both burst out laughing. It was about as genuine of a thank you as they'd ever heard out of Cory.

After the laughter stopped, Clacker said something else, directing it to Brad alone. Christy watched as Brad nodded. Then Clacker extended his right claw towards Brad who balled up his fist and tapped the creature's extended claw. The two bowed to each other. As they were getting back to stretching the fabric over the wings, Christy asked, "What did Clacker say to you?" When Brad ignored her, she squeezed his arm and tried again. "Please, Brad, tell me."

Brad stared at the ground and Christy wasn't sure he'd answer her, but finally he said, "You must watch over the one who looks like you but is not the same. He is angry but doesn't mean it." Then Brad fell silent.

CHAPTER 23

The wind was making the glider strain backwards against its rope ties. Despite the perfect fit of the fabric to the metal piping, the wind had been a problem, constantly blowing the fabric before they could even get it close to the frame. Eventually they were able to get it stretched over the wings, and they placed their packs in the seats just as Christy and Danny had done the year before.

Christy had already directed Cory and Brad to take their seats and was showing Clacker what she needed done. She and Danny would cut the ropes from the outside seats as Clacker pushed them forward against the wind. If everything went as planned, they would be propelled over the slab, down the wooden ramp, onto the crushed stone pathway, and out over the cliff's edge to a small island that was less than a football field away. Christy wasn't sure how it worked, but she knew that even though the wind was fierce against the wings and should logically push the glider backwards despite Clacker's efforts, somehow the wheels would harness the backwards thrust of the wind and translate that into forward movement.

As a last precaution, Christy walked with Clacker and showed him the edge of the path that the glider would take before taking off over the water. She pantomimed what they'd done last time, and as she was looking towards the island, she heard a sharp crack behind her. She looked at Clacker standing next to her. He staggered and stumbled towards the edge of the cliff. With her heart in her throat, she watched as he tumbled off into the raging water below.

Christy screamed and turned around to see four ancients surrounding the glider. She recognized Angry Ancient and also Protector and Neutral Ancient. The fourth one was not familiar to her. Angry Ancient was waving a pistol and grinning viciously. The ancient took a few steps toward Christy and pointed down at her. He seemed to be demanding that she come join the rest of them. Wiping her tears, she walked over to her companions.

As the four kids grouped together, an argument broke out among the ancients. Christy and the others could only watch, as none of them knew the language.

Protector Ancient pointed over the edge of the clearing towards the island and the gesture was met by nods from Neutral Ancient. Angry Ancient shook his head and pounded one fist into the other. Protector Ancient shouted above the wind and pointed again towards the edge of the clearing and the island beyond.

Then Angry Ancient violently brought his hands down and spread them out in a clear signal that he was saying no to Protector Ancient. The two arguing Ancients stood face to face, first one then the other screaming and gesturing. The kids were watching along with the unknown ancient and Neutral Ancient. As the argument became more animated, Brad stepped apart from the others. None of their captors paid any attention to him as he moved right between the two arguing ancients. All arguing stopped as Brad's presence took everyone by surprise.

He raised his arms up over his head and spoke in a loud voice. It wasn't English, and Christy was pretty sure he was speaking Ancient. Whatever it was, it was short— only a few words— but it certainly startled the ancients present.

Jack traveled all night until the reddish sun crested the horizon. He knew Christy and Clacker would be heading right for the Sacred Shrine clearing and the glider. But he also knew that TuMaz would follow them there.

As Jack approached the outskirts of the clearing, he became cautious. If the kids and TuMaz were all headed there, it wouldn't pay to stumble into a problem. He slowed down and followed parallel to the path using the tangled growth of plants and the scattered boulders for cover as he inched closer.

Just before he reached the vantage point, he looked down and smiled. Pressed into the spongy moss covering was the distinct impression of a human butt. Stuck to the moss inside the impression was a torn piece of a candy wrapper. The kids had been here. At that moment a shot carried on the wind back to him from the clearing and he heard a scream. It sounded like Christy!

Jack got on his stomach and slunk around the edge of the nearest boulder. He could hear everything fairly clearly since the wind was blowing every little utterance towards him. He was the closest to the clearing he could get without being seen. It was an advantage, but as of yet, he hadn't figured out how he could use it to influence the scene below. For the moment, the best thing he could do was watch and figure out what was going on. Christy, Danny and the Peters twins seemed to be under guard by his cellmates, his jailor, and TuMaz, who was brandishing one of his missing pistols. None of them seemed to be harmed, but Clacker was nowhere in sight. Jack's stomach knotted at what that might imply.

As he watched, he thought he saw Danny staring directly at him. After checking that none of the ancients were looking his way, he nodded with an exaggerated movement of his head. Danny responded in kind and Jack waited and watched. None of the ancients were paying any attention to Danny or looking towards Jack's hiding spot at all.

Something was going on down there that was coming to a head. TuMaz and CaTaz were arguing back and forth. It seemed as if it was about to escalate into violence between the arguing ancients, when one of the Peters twins stepped between TuMaz and CaTaz. To his amazement, Jack heard one of the Peters twins speak in Ancient, demanding to go home. The boy's comment startled the ancients. All of them stayed silent as they stared at the human who Jack knew had uttered an ancient rite: the Rite of Home. It meant that the Ancients had to let him go, let him use the glider.

Jack had to smile at the boy and his bravery, but TuMaz didn't look impressed.

Christy who'd witnessed the reaction of the ancients, asked, "Brad, what did you say?"

She had to tap his arm before he answered, but the ancients allowed them to talk, clearly still in shock and impressed with the boy.

"I said I want to go home. Christy, why can't we go home?"

Christy looked up at Protector Ancient and Neutral Ancient, and neither one would make eye contact with her. They looked uncomfortable with their spears pointed at the humans in front of them.

"Brad, listen to me," Christy began. "Can you speak their language enough to tell them something else, do you think?" Christy waited, then became frustrated when he didn't answer. She punched him in the arm.

"Can you speak their language?"

"Only a little from the video glass," he finally said, rubbing where she'd hit him.

Danny started to say something quietly, but Christy stopped him. She was trying to achieve something here, and it annoyed her that Danny had attempted to interrupt.

"Tell them it's our right to go. Just like before." She waited. Finally screaming at him, she said, "Brad! Tell them."

Brad cleared his throat and said something guttural that ended with a higher pitched few syllables. When he finished, Christy noticed Protector Ancient nodding slightly and hiding a smile from Angry Ancient.

"Can you use the word 'claim' or something like it?" Christy asked, punching him in the arm again.

Brad nodded.

"Good ... then say 'we claim our right to go.'"

Brad didn't move or say anything for a few seconds but then he stood up and bellowed out in a loud voice, looking directly towards the cliff edge and the island. He grunted, hissed and gestured with his whole being. When he was done, he sat down. Christy was about to ask him to repeat his performance when Danny grabbed her arm.

"Christy, there's something—"

"Do that again, Brad!" she said, ignoring Danny. "Please." She hit his arm again to prompt him and he complied.

Clearly, he'd impressed Protector and Neutral Ancient and the other ancient that Christy didn't know. They mumbled amongst themselves and said a few words to Angry Ancient.

Angry Ancient stared at Brad. When the other ancients again said something to him, he grabbed Brad by his arm and yanked him abruptly to his feet. Then he pulled the startled boy with him, heading off towards the cliff's edge.

Christy and Danny both screamed in protest and Cory stood up to run after his brother, but the spears came down crossing in front of them and even though the eyes of the remaining ancients showed sympathy, they didn't let anyone go after Angry Ancient or Brad, who was now crying.

Danny stood up, ignoring the spears and said to Christy, "I'm going to run, try to stop them from catching me."

Christy had no time to ask what he meant, and he didn't explain, just dashed off in the opposite direction from where Angry Ancient and Brad were headed.

The three ancients still guarding were caught by surprise, but only for a second. Neutral Ancient started after Danny, but Christy was ready for him.

She tackled him around his legs and it so startled him that he dropped his spear as he lurched forward.

As Christy and Neutral Ancient tumbled to the ground, she heard Danny yell, "Jack, here, take this!"

She rolled over to see Danny throwing something high into the air. Bolting out of a hiding place still yards away and reaching up to grab what Danny had thrown was her grandfather.

Jack adjusted the pistol in his hand as TuMaz continued to drag the boy towards the edge of the sheer cliff. Jack guessed what the ancient was going to do. He ran closer and shouted in ancient as loud as he could, hoping his voice would carry against the wind. Jack was rewarded when TuMaz turned around.

"You goat, I'll shoot you now, let the boy go!" Jack shouted.

TuMaz smiled cruelly and almost as if he had seen it done in a movie, the ancient pulled the struggling boy tighter to him and placed the pistol to his head. TuMaz responded, almost quietly, his voice carrying on the wind towards the humans and his companions, loud and clear.

"I will kill this one."

Jack shouted again, knowing that to be heard he'd have to almost scream. The wind was against him. A whisper from TuMaz would make it back to him in all its clarity but for him to be heard by TuMaz, he was going to have to keep shouting. But Jack wasn't trying to be heard by TuMaz.

Switching to English, Jack shouted, "Peters boy, do as I say." He stared straight at TuMaz.

Danny caught on and said, "He's Brad."

Jack nodded. "Brad," he shouted in English, "use your leg. Stick it between his legs and then push him if he drops his pistol even for a second."

Everyone was standing still, Jack with the pistol he had trained on TuMaz and TuMaz with Jack's other pistol pressed against Brad's temple. Everyone else was watching, helplessly.

Suddenly, an idea struck him, and Jack lowered his pistol.

Reverting to ancient again, he said, "So, it seems we are at a stalemate." Jack tucked his pistol into his belt, hoping it would have the desired effect.

For almost the count of ten, Jack thought it wasn't going to work, but then TuMaz relaxed, lowering the pistol.

Brad was quick. He stuck his leg in between TuMaz's legs and leaned in, giving the startled ancient a shove. Both of them began to tumble over. TuMaz let go of the boy and the pistol in order to break his fall, and Brad rolled clear and started to scramble away. TuMaz rose rapidly to his knees and reached for the pistol, a few feet away.

Before the ancient could even touch the pistol, Jack drew and shot. TuMaz screamed in pain and clutched his arm to his chest. He doubled over in pain, writhing on the ground. Jack slowly came towards him and picked up his other pistol.

"Get up, you goat, I just nicked you."

The ancient stood up, holding his arm to stem the bleeding. Jack called back to Christy.

"Honey, you must have some rope with you, I'm guessing. Bring it here so I can tie this one up."

Christy slid her backpack off and knelt down, quickly rummaged through it, found some rope and jumped back up, sprinting over to her grandfather.

Jack busied himself, first with making sure that the wound wasn't serious—but it really was minor— and then with tying up the ancient. The other ancients were not going to be a problem, now that TuMaz, or 'Angry Ancient,' as Christy called him, was no longer in charge.

CHAPTER 24

Christy wiped her eyes with her sleeve and turned to speak, her voice thick with emotion. "Grandpa, you have to come back with us, please."

They were all clustered around in a circle next to Angry Ancient. Christy and Danny had filled Jack in on their trip up to the present point and explained about all they had discovered. They'd even shown him the devices and some of the glass plates. And they'd all grieved for Clacker as well. Christy's grandfather had wept too, unashamed. Until then, they hadn't a second to even think of their friend's death.

"I don't know, honey," Jack said, struggling to speak through his grief. "After hearing from CaTaz what this goat here plans to do," he said, kicking TuMaz's boot, "I don't think I can. He's put in motion a war to rid this world of Cleaners. I think I owe it to Clacker to find his family and let them know. From what I can understand though, CaTaz and the others here will let you go. It seems that Brad invoked something called the Rite of Home without knowing."

"I think Brad probably did know, Grandpa," Christy said. She turned and smiled at Brad, who for the briefest moment returned her look before averting his eyes again. "But what is the Rite of Home?" she asked.

"According to CaTaz, it goes back thousands of years to when the ancients came and went between worlds through the portals. Apparently anytime they needed to, they could invoke the 'Rite of Home' and whoever was blocking their passage would allow them to return to their home world here. They have a lot of superstitions that revolve around protecting a creature's right to return home, which I guess is why, when you used the glider the first time, CaTaz gave you passage through the portal."

Jack paused, then added, "I think he kind of admires your spunk, Christy. All of you," he said, looking at each of them.

Christy began to cry again, upset that it seemed she would be unable to convince her grandfather to come with them. Jack came over and wrapped his arms around her.

"I promise to get back home to Earth as soon as I can, right after I find Clacker's family and tell them what has happened and what this council of ancients is planning. I have to stay and do that for Clacker, honey."

Christy was about to protest, but truthfully, she understood. Finally, she said, "Grandpa, there's something I realized a couple of days ago. That machine filled place we told you about … while we were there, I realized why your portal probably stopped working years ago. I'm not sure but I think it's because you removed the crystals from the water. Everything we've seen here is powered by those crystals. It has to be that."

Her grandfather smiled sadly at her. "I know. I came to the same conclusion during my time in prison in the village. I had a lot of time to think." He patted Christy on the shoulder. "Now we have to get you all on this glider and across. You won't be bothered by anyone this time, so you'll have all the time it takes for the portal to be activated by a storm in France.

"CaTaz and the rest of my friends here have given you some more food, just in case it takes a few days. Not that you weren't prepared," he said, ruffling Danny's hair. "Let's get everything together and get you on there."

Suddenly, a scream came from the glider. "Help!" Cory shrieked. They all turned and saw Cory dangling in the air. He was being lifted by the glider, which was still partially tied to its base slab, the wind trying to carry it aloft, a loose tie-down flapping wildly. As the glider reached its tethered end, it jerked abruptly.

Cory lost his grip and plunged down onto the granite slab, his back hitting the edge of the side of the block. He screamed as he bounced awkwardly down to the ground.

Christy was the first one to him as he lay moaning on the ground. Jack hurried over, yelling as he did.

"Don't touch him! I saw the way he hit that slab."

Jack knelt down next to the barely conscious boy.

"Cory, can you hear me?" he asked. Cory groaned. "Cory, can you hear me?" he asked again.

"Yes," Cory moaned. He had split his lip when he hit the ground, and blood was beginning to flow down his neck.

"What can I do?" Christy asked, feeling helpless.

"Do you have a clean cloth in your pack?" Jack asked. But Danny was already snapping into action. He had a cloth out and was unscrewing his canteen top even before the answer came out of the older man's mouth.

Cory was still moaning; his arms were shaking violently, and he had his eyes shut tight. Christy's grandfather pried his eyes open to look at his pupils. Satisfied, he accepted the wet cloth that Danny handed him and began to clean up and stop the flow of blood from the boy's lip.

While the three of them looked after Cory, Brad was turned away, mumbling to himself with his arms tightly hugged around his torso as he rocked on his heels. The ancients busied themselves with setting the glider back in its place after making sure it was undamaged. They secured it, and stood off, leaving the humans to themselves.

After half an hour or so, Cory's moaning stopped, and his breathing became more normal. He seemed to be starting to drift in and out of consciousness.

"Cory?" Jack yelled. "Do you hear me?"

Cory nodded slightly.

"Can you move your arms for me?"

Cory clenched his fists and bent his arms at the elbows, crying out as he did so.

"Good, can you move your legs?"

When Cory didn't respond, Jack asked again, "Cory, can you move your legs for me?"

"I ... can't," Cory whispered. "I don't know where they are. I can't feel them."

Christy looked to her grandfather and saw that he was tearing up.

"Cory has probably broken his back, honey," he said.

"What do we do?" Christy asked, beginning to sob.

"We have to get him home somehow. He won't be able to get any help in this world, I'm afraid," Jack stated. "I'll have to go with you, to try to stabilize his back on the glider and to carry him through the portal and out of the water on the other side in France. You kids can't be expected to do that. He'd drown without being able to use his legs."

As scared and sad as Christy felt, a little thrill went through her as her grandfather announced his decision to come home with them. But they still had to get Cory to the island without causing more damage to his spine.

While Jack was comforting Cory and making sure he stayed awake, they heard a large explosion.

"What was that?" Christy asked, jumping up and heading towards the cliff's edge where the sound had come from.

As soon as the explosion happened, Angry Ancient began to laugh. "You all lose," he said in English, cackling delightedly. "I have had your way home destroyed."

On the island, the door to the portal was shattered and the hill was collapsed in. The explosion had destroyed their only realistic hope of returning home. Christy couldn't believe what she was seeing. Her legs drained of their strength and she lowered herself to her knees.

Danny came up beside her, and seeing the devastation, covered his face with his hands as if to block out the dreadful sight. Jack and the ancients also rushed to the edge, leaving Brad kneeling over his brother. When Christy turned back to look at the twins, she screamed.

"Angry Ancient is gone!"

CaTaz and PeSaz scrambled to attention and scanned the clearing, looking for a trail to follow. Jack spoke rapidly in ancient and the two stopped short, nodding at him, but seeming more solemn and deflated for it. "I told them to let him go," Christy's grandfather explained. He spit on the ground and kicked at the dirt, venting his anger on the soil.

"He must have had a knife hidden somewhere," Jack said. "I don't know how he managed to have the portal blown up, but now we have no way of getting back without returning to my place and hoping that we're right about the crystals."

"How do we get Cory back there?" Danny asked.

"Maybe we could make a cart of some kind and push him there on it," Jack replied. He looked down at Cory, who was still semiconscious, and stepped back from him, motioning the others over just in case Cory could focus enough to listen.

"I don't think he'd make it back to my portal. We have no way of knowing what sort of internal damage he might have beyond the broken back. If he can't move or feel his legs, his spinal cord is either severed or severely compressed. He needs to get home as soon as possible."

"We have to try, don't we Grandpa?"

Jack nodded. "Yes, honey. We do have to try. We don't have any other alternatives but to head back to my portal and try to get it working. Hopefully it won't take too long. Time may be of the essence."

"I— I stole some of my mom's antibiotics to pack away in case of a bad cut or something," Danny said sheepishly. "I think we ought to start giving those to Cory if he's able to swallow."

"Bless you, Danny," Christy's grandfather replied. "That just may help get Cory through this."

Jack motioned to his two ancient friends and they spoke in whispers together. After conferring with them, he said, "My friends will help us get back to my place. They either can't or won't go back to their village."

"Grandpa," Christy began, sensing an opportunity, "you have to come with us. It's too dangerous here now for you."

"I'll help bring Cory to my portal. We'll see over the next day if that attempt can even be made. It all depends on what other than his back may be wrong.

"If we can set out and if we get Cory back to my portal, and if he's not fighting fever or something worse, it will mean he's stable enough for you kids to handle going through the portal with him. Let's hope. But those are all big 'ifs.'

"I was very worried about the glider ride. I don't think you kids could have used the glider and kept him stable and safe, but that's out of the question now." Jack paused, and looked down at Cory a few feet away, then said, "I haven't had a chance to let it sink in, but I'm going to miss Clacker. After hearing what he did to come with you all the way here, I owe it to his family and species to stay and warn them."

Brad, who had seemed to be oblivious to everything they'd been discussing, put himself directly in front of Christy and blurted out, "Cory needs to get home now. I want to go home too. Christy, can we go home now?"

Christy took a deep breath and answered him as best she could. "We have a long way to go, Brad. Do you remember when you and Danny first got here? We have to head back there before we can go home."

Brad stood still, frowning and acting as if he'd not even heard her. "Cory can't wait. I can't wait if Cory can't wait. Christy, Cory isn't well. We need to get him home. Cory can't wait."

"Brad, we have to wait. Yes, he's in trouble, but we have no choice. We will take him with us for as long as it takes."

Brad seemed to become more agitated, rocking on his heels, his breath coming out in whistling ragged streams. He hugged himself as they'd seen him do numerous times, while he mumbled.

"Cory can't wait. Why do we have to wait?" he said repeatedly.

All except Jack watched Brad pacing and mumbling. Jack had knelt back down and was stroking Cory's hair, and repeatedly wetting a cloth to keep his chin and lip clean.

Brad suddenly stopped his pacing and rushed over to the pile of backpacks and began to open them one by one.

"Brad?" Christy asked. "What are you doing?"

Brad dove into each backpack, flinging things out, and scattering their contents all over the ground in his focused haste. Pulling the brass devices from each pack, he placed them along with the four silver, cup-like vessels on the ground next to his brother.

Separating the four silver cups, he carefully paced off each one, counting steps out loud and nodding to himself as he placed them in a square surrounding his brother.

Pulling four crystals from his pocket, he snapped one into each metal vessel. Then he took each of the brass devices and made them spring up to the open position. Christy watched in awe as he put crystals into each of the four devices.

"We're going home. Cory has to go home, now," Brad said.

Christy shrugged and shook her head.

They all watched as Brad took the four devices and placed them side by side. He joined them all together and placed them just outside of the imaginary square he'd built around his brother.

Brad stood up and looked at the others, who all stared at what he'd just done.

"Hurry, Cory has to go home."

"What do you want, Brad?" Christy asked, feeling helplessly confused.

Suddenly Danny snapped his fingers. "I get it!" he exclaimed. "Christy, get in the square next to Cory. Quickly!"

Brad smiled and nodded without lifting his eyes from the ground. He knelt next to the device he'd removed the crystal from and waited. Christy caught on and in the thrill of excitement, managed to smile. Instead of immediately joining Danny and Cory, she turned to her grandfather. He had knelt down next to Cory, apparently comprehending Brad's plan, and resigning himself to helping. Christy was momentarily thrilled, until she thought of Clacker.

"Brad, can you swim?" When he didn't answer she repeated herself, yelling this time, "Can you swim?"

Brad nodded, and Christy tapped her grandfather on the shoulder.

"Danny and I can help Cory if we come up through our pond, or the one in France. He won't drown. You need to stay and help any Cleaners you can."

Jack nodded grimly and stepped away from Cory and out of the square that Brad had made.

"Wait," Christy said, giving her grandfather a final hug.

After Christy let her grandfather go and joined Danny and Cory, Brad reset the crystal in the fourth device and stood next to it for a second.

"Brad, hurry!" Christy said.

Brad waited as the power hummed. All at once a wall of light shot up and connected the four corners surrounding the kids. When it was higher than all their heads, Brad quickly separated the four devices, which had no effect on the pulsating light. He collapsed them and cradled them in his arms as he joined his brother and friends.

Christy waved one last time to her grandfather as the world dissolved around them.

CHAPTER 25

Christy and Danny were both holding onto Cory. They came out under water only a few feet from the surface, and dog paddled to shore, dragging Cory between them. Brad, who was clutching the devices in his left hand, made it to land one handed as well. Thankfully, they had come up in Christy's pond, not in France.

"Stay with Cory," Christy called out behind her, as she sprinted up to the house.

She tried opening the door, but it was locked. Fumbling for the key in its secret spot beneath the doormat, she unlocked the door and burst through.

"Mom! Dad!" The house was dark and silent. She raced upstairs and back down, calling every few seconds. Getting no response, she grabbed the phone and dialed 911.

"Hey, how are you?" Christy asked, poking her head into Cory's hospital room. Cory's mom was sitting next to his bed and seemed surprised to see Christy, but she nodded quickly and excused herself as Christy awkwardly settled on the edge of Cory's bed.

"Ok, I guess ... you?"

"Back to normal," she said.

"Back to normal," Cory repeated, and shook his head. "Normal for you isn't going to be normal for me anymore, Walker."

Christy squirmed. She knew she couldn't say anything that would help, so she just sat in silence.

"Is everybody back from France?" Cory asked.

Christy shook her head. "My parents took a later flight than yours did. They're due in tonight. Mrs. Lake is driving me to the airport to meet them." She added, "Brad says to say hi."

Cory snorted. "That's bull, he's never said hello to me before. But I'm not surprised he's not here. He never has been able to enter a hospital, even for me I guess."

"He saved all of us, you know."

"I know." Cory looked away. "I was pretty much out of it there for the last hour or so. What did you tell the ambulance people?"

"I said you slipped on the dock and hit your back real hard."

"So those brass things made a portal that got us home?"

"Yeah. Brad saw how they worked by looking at all those glass plate videos. Use the right world and solar system devices with a portal one, and you don't need a body of water. Although we came up through my pond."

"Where'd you hide them? I assume you did."

Christy smiled slightly. "Yeah, while I waited with you and Brad, I had Danny hide them. We didn't mention to anyone how we got home. Everybody thinks that we got my grandfather's portal working again."

Cory nodded. "Did your grandfather come back with us?"

Christy shook her head. "He needs to warn the Cleaners about Angry Ancient's vendetta against them."

"At least you know he's alive and well."

"There's that," she said quietly. "How long are they going to keep you?"

"A few more days then I go in for surgery to stabilize the spine. Nothing they can do to get my legs back, but they want to make sure it's going to heal ok. Then they want me to go to a rehab hospital in Boston for a while."

Christy nodded along, and they talked for a few more minutes. "I'm sorry, Cory," she said finally.

Cory stared at her for a second then turned his head away again with tears in his eyes.

"Please leave," he said as he buried his head into the pillow. Christy almost said something else, but it was easier not to, so she left, passing Cory's mother on her way out of the room.

Once out of the hospital, she breathed a sigh of relief. That was over. Now all she wanted to do was see her mom and dad.

Christy waited with Mrs. Lake and Danny just outside the security area at the airport as passengers hurried by off the plane from Paris. Finally, she saw her mom turning the corner and exiting past the bored security guard. Christy ran towards her.

"Mom!"

Her mom spotted her and dropped her luggage at her feet, opening her arms. As the two came together in a hug, they both began to cry. As Christy stepped back a foot or two, Danny gave Connie a hug too. Christy was smiling, then she frowned.

She looked around at the other passengers and people greeting them and couldn't spot her father.

"Where's dad?"

Her mom motioned them all over to a quieter spot with a circular bench, off to the side. She sat down and patted the spot next to her for Christy to take it. When Christy sat down, her mom took her hands and began.

"I don't know exactly where he is, honey. He and Detective Lockhart crossed into the Empty World going after you kids. They haven't come back yet. That's why I didn't come back when the Peters and Katie did."

Christy pulled her hands out of her mom's. "No! Why?"

"Why? What did you think we would do when you disappeared again?"

"We had no choice, Mom. Brad jumped in."

"You did have a choice. Danny could have woken up his mom," Connie said, nodding at Katie. "And you could have come right into our room when Cory came to you."

"Danny couldn't let Brad jump and get there by himself, you know that."

Her mom breathed deeply.

"Maybe I can understand that, but you should have made better choices. If you'd woken us up, your dad could have gone with you instead of Cory."

Christy began to cry. "I know. Cory will never walk again. And now dad is there. He doesn't know the portal that comes back to France is gone, and grandpa is the only one who is there who—"

Christy stopped and realized she was about to say that the portal wasn't really working yet, but that would prompt questions about how they'd all gotten home. So, she pretended to need a moment to compose herself before continuing.

"... who knows we got grandpa's portal working again. Dad and the Detective will be long gone from there by now, on their way to a portal that doesn't work." Christy stopped crying and wiped her eyes. "Mom, I have to go back, now. Who else will know what to do?"

"Christy, I can't let you go back, you know that."

"You'll have to lock me up then," Christy said through her tears, looking her mom sternly in the face, "because I'm going. Dad needs me."

Thanks for reading!

You made it to the end! This may be the end of the series story, but if you like reading the Empty World Saga, there's a special bonus.

Email insiders get the subscriber-exclusive short story about how Christy and Trevor save the holidays with the help from some Empty World technology.

Sign up for the my Email Insiders club and get *Christy's Risky Recipe* at:
www.davidkanderson.info

Books by David K. Anderson

Empty World Saga

All 5 books of of the Empty World Saga are available in ebook, paperback, hardcover, and audiobook.

1. Portal Through the Pond
2. Beyond the Portal
3. At the Portal's End
4. The Lost Portal
5. Portals in Peril

Read about the *Empty World Saga* and discover where to buy at: emptyworldsaga.com

About the Author

Growing up, David K. Anderson was mentored by his Uncle Ralph, a gifted artist who taught him to express himself in creative ways: writing, drawing and sculpting.

David is married and has three adult children. Throughout his adult life, he has volunteered countless hours with children with disabilities involving creative activities. His lifelong passions for art, sculpting and storytelling have helped him combine his talents to create enjoyment for hundreds of children of all abilities. His family's mutual love for fantasy, fiction, and fun along with a desire to ensure that children of all abilities can be heroes, has motivated him to write stories that engage us all.

59190203R00143

Made in the USA
Columbia, SC
31 May 2019